JUST WILLIAM AT SCHOOL

RELUCTANTLY WILLIAM CAME UP TO THE FRONT OF THE CLASS.
THERE HE STOOD, PURPLE WITH ANGER AND EMBARRASSMENT,
GLARING FEROCIOUSLY AT THE MASTER.

(see page 127)

RICHMAL CROMPTON

Just William
at
School

Illustrated by Thomas Henry

MACMILLAN
CHILDREN'S BOOKS

First published 1997 by Macmillan Children's Books
a division of Macmillan Publishers Limited
25 Eccleston Place, London SW1W 9NF
Basingstoke and Oxford
www.macmillan.com

Associated companies throughout the world

ISBN 0 333 71235 8

7 9 8 6

A CIP catalogue record for this book is available from
the British Library.

Phototypeset by Intype London Ltd
Printed and bound in Great Britain by
Mackays of Chatham PLC, Kent

CONTENTS

CHAPTER ONE

FINDING A SCHOOL FOR WILLIAM

WILLIAM'S SUSPICIONS WERE first aroused by the atmosphere of secrecy that enveloped the visit of Mr Cranthorpe-Cranborough. Mr Cranthorpe-Cranborough was a very distant cousin of William's father (so many times removed as to be almost out of sight) and was coming to stay for a week-end with the Browns. William gathered that his father had not met Mr Cranthorpe-Cranborough before in spite of the relationship, that the visitor was self-invited, and that the visit was in some way connected with himself. He gathered this last fact from whispered confabulations between his family during which they watched him in that way in which whispering confabulators always watch those who are the subject of the whispered confabulations.

William, while keeping eyes and ears alert, pretended to be sublimely unaware of all this. He went his way with an air of unsuspecting innocence that lured his family into a false security. "Fortunately," his mother whispered very audibly to Ethel once as he was just going out of the room, "William hasn't the slightest idea what he's coming for."

Meanwhile beneath William's exaggerated air of

1

guilelessness William's mind worked fast. Whenever he came upon any scattered twos he put them together to make four. These fours he stored up in mind as he went his way, apparently absorbed in his games, the well-being of his mongrel Jumble, the progress of his tamed caterpillars and earwigs, the shooting properties of his new bow and arrows, and the activities of his friends the Outlaws. But there was no look or sign or whisper from the grown-up world around him that the seemingly unconscious William did not intercept and store up for future reference. William, as some people had been known to put it, was "deep".

"Yes, dear," said Mrs Brown to Ethel, her nineteen-year-old daughter, "he's going to arrive before tea and your father's going to try to get home for tea, and they're going to talk it over together quietly after tea in the morning-room."

"Oh, well, I shall be busy," said Ethel, "I shall be helping Moyna Greene with her dress for the fancy dress ball, so I shan't be in their way. She's going as a lady of Elizabethan times and she's going to look *sweet*."

"I expect they'd like to be left alone to talk things over . . . Sh!" as she perceived William who had heard every word lolling negligently in the doorway cracking nuts.

"Well, William," brightly, "had a nice afternoon?"

"Yes, thanks," said William.

"We were just talking about Ethel's friend, Miss Greene, who's going to a fancy dress ball."

"Yes, I heard you," said William.

"She's going as a lady of the fourteenth century," proceeded Mrs Brown still brightly.

"Uh – huh," said William without interest as he cracked another nut.

Some of Mrs Brown's brightness faded.

"*William!*" she said indignantly, "*do* stop dropping shells on to the carpet."

"A'right – sorry," said William, stolidly turning to go away and cracking another nut.

"His *manners!*" said Ethel, elevating her small and pretty nose in disgust.

"Yes, dear," said Mrs Brown soothingly, "but *we* needn't bother about them *now*."

William wandered out into the garden. Though he did not for a minute cease his consumption of nuts he grew yet more thoughtful. He was beginning to look forward to the projected visit of Mr Cranthorpe-Cranborough with distinct apprehension. Whatever it boded, William felt sure that it boded no good to him. Still cracking nuts with undiminished energy and leaving a little trail of broken shells to mark his track over the immaculate lawn (and incidentally to make the gardener rise to dazzling heights of eloquence when he tried to mow it the next morning) William withdrew to the strip of untended shrubbery at the bottom of the garden, and, sitting down upon a laurel bush, began thoughtfully to throw pebbles at the next door cat who was its only other occupant. The next door cat, who looked upon William's pebble-throwing as a sign of his affection, began to purr loudly . . .

William considered the situation. This Mr Cranthorpe-Cranborough was coming for some sinister purpose tomorrow. That sinister purpose must at all costs be frustrated. But first of all he must find out what that sinister purpose was ... He threw another handful of nut shells at the next door cat. The next door cat purred still more loudly ... The visitor was going to have a quiet little talk with his father after tea tomorrow ... By hook or by crook William decided to hear that quiet little talk. The only drawback to the plan was that the morning-room contained no possible place of concealment for eavesdroppers ...

"William dear, this is Mr Cranthorpe-Cranborough, a relation of ours who has come to pay us a little visit," said Mrs Brown.

William looked up.

The first thing that struck you about Mr Cranthorpe-Cranborough was his bigness, and the second was his smile. Mr Cranthorpe-Cranborough's smile was as large and full as himself. His teeth were so over-crowded that when he smiled it almost seemed as if some were in danger of dropping out. He placed a large hand upon William's head.

"So *this* is the little man," he said.

"Uh-huh?" said William.

"Oh, his *manners*," groaned Ethel turning her eyes towards the sky.

"A-ha," said Mr Cranthorpe-Cranborough, smiling like a playful ogre, "you may safely leave his manners to *me*. I'm used to teaching little boys their manners."

William took a nut out of his pocket and cracked it.

"William!" groaned Mrs Brown.

4

William took out a handful of nuts and handed it to Mr Cranthorpe-Cranborough.

"Have one?" he said politely.

"Er – no, I thank you," said Mr Cranthorpe-Cranborough. Then he smiled the very full smile again, "But I'd like a talk with you, my little man."

His little man turned a sphinx-like countenance to him and cracked another nut.

"How far have you got in Arithmetic?" asked Mr Cranthorpe-Cranborough.

"Uh-huh?" said William.

Ethel groaned.

"Fractions?" suggested Mr Cranthorpe-Cranborough.

William's whole attention was given to the inside of the nut that he had just cracked.

"Bad!" he said indignantly, "an' I paid twopence for 'em . . . I'll take it back to the shop."

"Decimals?" said Mr Cranthorpe-Cranborough.

"No, Brazils," said William succinctly.

"I think perhaps it would be better if we left them," murmured Mrs Brown faintly, and she and Ethel departed, Ethel murmuring wildly, "His *manners!*"

"And what about History?" said Mr Cranthorpe-Cranborough.

William, investigating another nut, seemed to have no views on history.

Mr Cranthorpe-Cranborough cleared his throat, smiled his large fat smile and said, "Ha!" to attract William's attention. He failed, however. William's whole attention was given to throwing bits of his bad nut at the next door cat who had disappeared at the first intrusion of the grown-ups, but had now returned and was again purring loudly.

"What are the dates of Queen Elizabeth?" said Mr Cranthorpe-Cranborough.

"Uh?" said William absently, "here's another of 'em bad an' chargin' *twopence* for 'em! Haven't they gotta *nerve!*"

Mr Cranthorpe-Cranborough gave up the attempt.

"I'm going to have a nice little talk with your father after tea, my little man," he said.

William cracked a nut in (partial) silence and threw the shells at the cat. Then he said casually, "I s'pose they've told you he's deaf? He gets awful mad if people don't shout loud enough. You've gotta shout *awful* loud to make him hear."

"Er – your mother never mentioned it," said Mr Cranthorpe-Cranborough taken aback.

"No," said William mysteriously, "an' don't say anythin' about it to her or to any of them. They don' like folks mentionin' it. They're – they're – sort of sens'tive about it."

"Oh!" said Mr Cranthorpe-Cranborough still more taken aback. Then he recovered himself. "Now let's have a few dates," he said briskly.

"Yes, dates is more sense," said William with interest, "you can look at 'em before you buy 'em to see if they're bad. That's the worst of nuts. You can't see 'em through the shells."

Viciously he threw the defaulting nut at the cat who remembered suddenly a previous engagement on the other side of the fence and disappeared.

While Mr Cranthorpe-Cranborough was engaged in

recovering himself for a fresh assault upon William's ignorance Ethel appeared.

"Will you come in to tea now?" she said to the visitor with a sweet smile.

Mr Cranthorpe-Cranborough responded to the best of his ability with his fullest smile.

William, interested by the phenomenon, went up to his bedroom to practise, but found that he had not enough teeth to get the full effect.

When he descended he found his father in the hall hanging up his coat and hat.

"You're back early, father, aren't you?" said William innocently.

"With your usual intelligence, my son," said William's father, "you have divined aright . . . Where's Mr What's-his-name?"

"Having tea in the drawing-room, father," said William.

Mr Brown went into the morning-room. William followed him.

"Have you – met him?" said Mr Brown.

"Yes," said William.

"Er – do you like him?"

"He's very deaf," said William.

"Deaf?"

"Yes . . . you've gotta shout ever so hard to make him hear."

"Good Heavens!" groaned Mr Brown.

"An' *he* shouts very hard, too, like what deaf people do, you know, with not hearin' themselves – but he dun't

like you *sayin'* anythin' about him bein' deaf, but he likes
you jus' shoutin'. They're havin' their tea now. He's given
'em quite sore throats already."

Mr Brown groaned again but at that minute entered
Mrs Brown and the guest. She performed a rapid intro-
duction and departed. William had already disappeared.
He had gone round to the front lawn and was sitting there
leaning against the house cracking nuts. Just above his
head was the open window of the morning-room. It was
not possible from that position to overhear a conversation
carried on in normal voices in the morning-room, but
William hoped that he had assured that this conversation
would be carried on in abnormal voices. His hopes were
justified. His father's voice raised to a bellow reached
him.

"Won't you sit down?"

And Mr Cranthorpe-Cranborough's in a hoarse shout:
"Thanks so much."

"Now about this school—" yelled his father.

"Exactly," bellowed Mr Cranthorpe-Cranborough. "I
hope to open it in the spring. I should like to include your
son among the first numbers – special terms of course."

There was a pause, then William's father spoke in a
voice of thunder.

"Very good of you."

"Not at all," bellowed Mr Cranthorpe-Cranborough.

"He's – perhaps I'd better prepare you . . ." boomed
Mr Brown's voice making the very window panes rattle
in their frames, "he – he doesn't quite conform to type.
He's a bit – individualistic."

Mr Cranthorpe-Cranborough drew in his breath, then
with a mighty effort bellowed:

"But he ought to conform to type. It's only a matter of training . . . I'm most anxious to include your son on our roll when we open next spring."

Purple in the face Mr Brown yelled:

"Very good of you."

William, whose conscience never allowed him to do any more eavesdropping than was absolutely necessary to his plans, arose and thoughtfully cracking his last nut, walked round the house. At the side door he came across his mother and Ethel clinging together in terror.

"What *has* happened?" his mother was saying hysterically. "Why are they shouting at each other like that? What *has* happened?"

"They must be quarrelling!" groaned Ethel. A re-echoing bellow from Mr Brown (who was really only saying, "Very good of you" again) made the house shake and Ethel screamed, "They'll be *fighting* in a minute . . . What *shall* we do?"

Mrs Brown noticed William and made an effort to control herself.

"Where are you going, William?"

William, his hands deep in his pockets, answered nonchalantly. "Down to the village to buy a stick of liquorice," he said.

He walked down to the village very thoughtfully.

So *that* was it . . . they were going to send him to that man's school, were they? Huh! . . . *were* they? William for one had made up his mind that they were not, but just for a minute he was not sure how he could prevent them. Silently he considered various plans. None seemed suitable. Open opposition was, he knew, useless. In open opposition he had no chance against his family. But there must surely be other ways . . .

Mrs Brown had once stayed in Eastbourne where she had watched a neat little crocodile of neat little boys walking in a straight and tidy line past her house every day and the sight had impressed her. The thought of William walking like that – a neat and tidy component of a neat and tidy line talking politely to his partner, keeping just behind the boy in front, with plastered hair and shiny shoes, walking sedately – was an alluring and startling picture when compared with the William of the present, leaping over fences, diving into ditches, shinning up trees, dragging his toes in the dust, shouting . . . Mrs Brown had a vague idea that some mysterious change of spirit came over a boy on entering the portals of a boarding-school transforming him from a young savage to a perfect little gentleman, and she would have liked to see this change take place in William. Moreover Mr Cranthorpe-Cranborough had distinctly mentioned "special fees".

Mr Brown had no very strong feelings on the subject. He was prepared to leave it all to his wife. The only two people concerned who had any very strong feelings about it were Mr Cranthorpe-Cranborough and William. Mr Cranthorpe-Cranborough wanted to fill his new school. He did not consider William to be very promising material but he couldn't afford at the present juncture to be too particular about material . . . And William had very strong feelings on the subject indeed. William could not even contemplate life divorced from the beloved fields and woods of his native village, his beloved Outlaws and Jumble his mongrel.

*

On returning home William found his father in the hall.

"What the dickens do you mean," said his father irritably and hoarsely, "by telling me the fellow was deaf? He's no more deaf than I am."

William opened wide eyes of innocent surprise.

"Isn't he, father?" he said, "I'm awfully sorry."

William's father, upon whom William's looks of innocence and surprise were always completely wasted, moved his hand to his throat with an involuntary spasm of pain.

"No, he isn't," he said brokenly, "and you knew perfectly well he wasn't. Your over-exuberant sense of humour needs a little pruning, my boy, and if I hadn't got the worst sore throat I've had in years I'd prune it for you here and now."

William moved hastily out of the danger zone still murmuring apologies. He went to the morning-room where he found Mr Cranthorpe-Cranborough. Mr Cranthorpe-Cranborough addressed him, also brokenly.

"Your father doesn't seem to be very deaf, William," he whispered hoarsely, "I spoke to him in quite an ordinary tone of voice towards the end of our conversation and he seemed to hear all right."

William fixed unfaltering eyes upon him.

"Yes, then your voice must be the kind he hears nat'rul. He does hear some sorts nat'rul. He hears all ours nat'rul."

With this cryptic remark he withdrew leaving Mr Cranthorpe-Cranborough looking thoughtful.

The next morning Mr Cranthorpe-Cranborough asked William to go for a walk with him. "William and I," he said pleasantly to Mrs Brown, "must get to know each other."

William emerged from Mrs Brown's hands for the walk almost repellently clean and tidy. Mrs Brown was determined that William should make a good impression on Mr Cranthorpe-Cranborough.

For a time William walked in silence and Mr Cranthorpe-Cranborough talked. He talked about the glorious historical monuments of England and the joys of early rising and the fascination of decimals and H.C.F.'s and the beauty of all foreign languages. He warmed to William as he talked for William seemed to be drinking in his words almost avidly. William's solemn eyes never left his face. He could not know, of course, that William was not listening to a word he said but was engaged in trying to count his teeth . . .

"Now which of our grand national buildings have you seen?" said Mr Cranthorpe-Cranborough, returning to his first theme.

"Uh-huh?" said William who thought he'd got to thirty, but kept having to start again because they moved about so.

"I say, which of our grand national buildings have you seen?" said Mr Cranthorpe-Cranborough more distinctly.

"Oh," said William bringing his thoughts with an effort from Mr Cranthorpe-Cranborough's teeth to the less interesting one of our grand national buildings, "I've never been to races," said William sadly.

"Races?" said Mr Cranthorpe-Cranborough in surprise.

"Yes . . . you was talking about the Grand National, wasn't you?"

"Were, William, were," corrected Mr Cranborough.

"I'm not quite sure where," admitted William, "but I know a man what won some money on it last year."

"You misunderstand me, William," said Mr Cranborough rather irritably, "I'm referring to such places as Westminster Abbey and the Houses of Parliament."

"Oh," said William with waning interest, "I thought you was goin' to talk about racin'."

"Were, William, *were.*"

"At the Grand National."

"No, William ... no," he was finding conversation with William rather difficult, "have you never visited such places as Hampton Court?"

A gleam of interest came into William's face and he temporarily abandoned his self-imposed task of counting Mr Cranborough's teeth.

"Yes," he said, "I once went *there.* I remember 'cause there was a man there what told us it was haunted. Said a ghost of someone used to go downstairs there. Huh!"

William's final ejaculation was one of contemptuous amusement. But Mr Cranthorpe-Cranborough's face grew serious. His teeth receded from view almost entirely.

"No, no, William," he said reprovingly, "you must not make fun of such things. Indeed you must not. They are – they are not to be treated lightly. The fact that you have *seen* none is not proof that there *are* none ... far from it ... Believe me, William – though I have seen none myself I have friends who have."

"Didn't it scare 'em stiff?" said William with interest, and added dramatically, "rattlin' an' groanin' an' such-like."

Mr Cranborough was too much absorbed in his subject to correct William's phraseology.

"It does not – er – rattle or groan, William. It is the figure of a lady of the fifteenth century, and everyone does not see it. It is indeed a sinister omen to see it. Some evil always befalls those who see it. Sinister, William, means on the left hand, and used in the sense in which we use it, is a reference to the omens of the days of the Romans."

"Doesn't it *do* anythin' to 'em?" said William, disappointed by the lack of enterprise betrayed by the ghost, and left completely cold by the derivation of the word sinister.

"No," said Mr Cranborough, "it just *appears* – *but* the one who sees it, and only one person sees it on each occasion, invariably suffers some catastrophe. It is not wise, of course, to allow one's thoughts to *dwell* upon such things but it is not wise either to treat them entirely with contempt . . . Let us now turn our thoughts to brighter things . . . Do you keep a collection of – the flora of the neighbourhood, William?"

"No," admitted William, "I've never caught any of *them*. Didn't know there was any about. But I've got some caterpillars."

When William approached the morning-room just before lunch there were there his mother and Ethel and Robert, his grown-up brother. As William entered he heard his mother whisper:

"I think the time has come to tell him."

14

William entered, negligently toying with a handful of marbles.

"William," said his mother, "we have something to tell you."

"Uh-huh?" said William still apparently absorbed by his marbles.

"Oh, his *manners!*" groaned Ethel.

"This cousin of your father's," said his mother, "is really the headmaster of a boys' boarding-school and we *think* ... though nothing's yet arranged ... that we're going to send *you* to his school next spring. *Won't* it be nice?"

They all looked at William with interest to see how he should receive this startling news.

William received it as though it had been some casual comment on the weather.

"Uh-huh," he said absently, as he continued to toy negligently with his marbles.

He had the satisfaction of seeing his family thoroughly taken aback by his reception of the news.

He was very silent during lunch. He had not yet formed any definite plan of action beyond the negative plan of pretending to acquiesce. He could see that his attitude mystified them and the knowledge was a great consolation to him.

After lunch Mr Cranthorpe-Cranborough, who by now looked upon the addition of William's name to his roll of members as a certainty, went into the garden and Mrs Brown went to lie down. William, after strolling aimlessly about the house, joined Ethel in the drawing-room.

She was, however, not alone in the drawing-room. Moyna Greene in an elaborate fourteenth-century dress of purple and silver was with her.

"You look perfectly sweet, Moyna," Ethel was saying, "but I think the ruffle *does* want altering just here."

"I thought it did," said Moyna, "I'll do it now if I may. May I borrow your work basket? Thanks." She slipped off her ruffle.

"Let me help," said Ethel.

Just then the housemaid entered.

"Mrs Bott called to see you, Miss," she said to Ethel.

Ethel groaned and turned to Moyna.

"Oh, my dear . . . I'll be as quick as I can, but you know what she is . . . She'll keep me ages. You *won't* run away, will you?"

"No," promised the purple and silver vision.

"I'll tell you what you might do," said Ethel. "Go and let old Jenkins see you. I think he's in the greenhouse. I told him you were going as a fourteenth century lady and he said, 'Eh, her'll look rare prutty. I wish I could see her' – so he'd be so bucked if you would."

"All right," said Moyna, "I'll just finish this ruffle and then I'll go out to him."

"And I'll be as quick as I can," said Ethel, "but you know what she is."

William went quietly out of doors. His face was bright with inspiration and stern with resolve. First of all he satisfied himself that old Jenkins really was in the greenhouse.

Jenkins turned upon him as soon as he saw him in the doorway. Between old Jenkins and young William no love was lost.

16

"You touch one of my grapes, Master William," he said threateningly, "an' I'll tell your pa the minute he comes home tonight, I will. I grow these grapes for your ma an' pa – not you."

"I don' want any of your grapes, Jenkins," said William with a short laugh expressive of amused surprise at the idea. "Good gracious, what should *I* want with your ole grapes?"

Whereupon he departed with a swagger leaving old Jenkins muttering furiously, and went to join Mr Cranthorpe-Cranborough who was comfortably ensconced in a deck chair at the further end of the lawn wooing sleep. He had almost wooed it when William appeared and sat down noisily at his feet, and said in a tone that put any further wooing of sleep entirely out of the question:

"Hello, Mr Cranborough."

Mr Cranborough greeted William shortly and without enthusiasm. He did not want William. He did not like William. His interest in William began and ended with the special fees which he hoped William's parents might be induced to pay him – "special" in quite a different sense from the one in which Mrs Brown understood it. He had been quite happy without William and he meant his manner to convey this fact to William. But William was not sensitive to fine shades of manner.

"I've been thinkin'," he said slowly, "'bout what you said this mornin'."

"Ah," said Mr Cranthorpe-Cranborough, touched despite himself and thinking what a gift for dealing with the young he must possess to have made an impression upon such unpromising material as this boy's mind, and how one should never despair of material however unpromising.

"About what, my boy?" he said with interest, "the History? the French? the Arithmetic?"

"No," said William simply, "the ghost."

"Oh," said Mr Cranthorpe-Cranborough, "but – er – you should not allow your mind to *run* on such subjects, my boy."

"No," said William, "it's not runnin' on 'em. But I've just remembered somethin' about this house."

"What?" said Mr Cranthorpe-Cranborough.

William carefully selected a juicy blade of grass and began to chew it.

"Oh, it's prob'ly nothin'," he said carelessly, "but what you said this mornin' made me think of it, that's all."

William was adept at whetting people's curiosity.

"But what *was* it?" said Mr Cranthorpe-Cranborough irritably, "what *was* it?"

"Well, p'raps I'd better not mention it," said William, "you said we oughn't to let it run on our minds."

"I insist on your telling me," said Mr Cranthorpe-Cranborough.

"Oh, it's nothin' much," said William again, "only a sort of *story* about this house."

"*What* sort of a story?" insisted Mr Cranthorpe-Cranborough.

"Well," said William as though reluctantly, "some folks say that an ole house use to be here jus' where this house is now an' that a lady of the fourteenth century was killed in it once an' some folks say they've seen her. I don' b'lieve it," he ended carelessly, "*I've* never seen her."

18

Mr Cranthorpe-Cranborough's interest was aroused.

"What is this – this lady supposed to look like, my boy?" he said.

"She's dressed in purple and silver," said William, "with a long train an' a ruffle thing round her neck an' very black hair, and she's s'posed to walk out of that window over there," and he pointed to the drawing-room window, "and then go across the lawn behind those trees," he pointed to the trees which hid the greenhouse from view.

"And you say that people profess to have *seen* her?" said Mr Cranthorpe-Cranborough.

"Oh, yes," said William.

"And what does her coming portend?"

"Uh?" said William.

"What – what *happens* to those who see her?" repeated Mr Cranthorpe-Cranborough impatiently.

At that moment Miss Moyna Greene, having finished and donned the ruffle, stepped out of the drawing-room window on to the lawn in all her glory of purple and silver. Mr Cranthorpe-Cranborough gazed at her and his jaw dropped open.

"Look!" he gasped to William, "who's that?"

"Who's what?" said William gazing around innocently.

Miss Moyna Greene passed slowly to the middle of the lawn. Mr Cranthorpe-Cranborough's eyes, bulging with amazement, followed her. So did his trembling forefinger.

"There ..." he hissed, "just there."

William stared straight at Miss Moyna Greene.
"I don't see anyone," he said.

Drops of perspiration stood out on Mr Cranthorpe-Cranborough's brow. He took out a large silk handkerchief and mopped it. The figure of Miss Moyna Greene crossed the lawn and disappeared behind the trees...

Mr Cranthorpe-Cranborough gave a gasp.

MR CRANTHORPE-CRANBOROUGH GAZED ACROSS THE LAWN AND HIS JAW DROPPED. "LOOK!" HE GASPED TO WILLIAM. "WHO'S THAT?"

"Er – what did you say the – er – the sight of the vision is supposed to portend, William?" he said faintly. "What – what *happens* to those who see it?"

"Oh, I don' suppose anyone's really seen it," said William carelessly. "I never have. I think they've simply made it up – purple dress an' ruffle an' all – but it's *s'posed* to mean very bad luck for the one who sees it."

"W-w-what kind of bad luck?" stammered Mr Cranthorpe-Cranborough, whose ruddy countenance had faded to a dull grey.

"Well," said William confidentially, "it's s'posed to be seen by one of two people together an' the one what *sees* it is s'posed to be goin' to have some *very* bad luck *through* the other – the one what was with him when he saw it, but what didn't see it. The bad luck's s'posed always to come *through* the one what doesn't see it but what's *with* the one what *does*."

THE FIGURE OF MISS GREENE CROSSED THE LAWN AND
DISAPPEARED BEHIND THE TREES.

Through the trees William spied the figure of Miss Moyna Greene who had evidently left Jenkins and was returning to the drawing-room.

"An' folks *say*," added William carelessly, "that it's worst of *all* if you see it twice – once going from the house and once comin' to it."

The figure of Miss Moyna Greene emerged from the trees and passed slowly on to the lawn. Mr Cranthorpe-Cranborough watched it in stricken silence. Then he said to William with an unconvincing attempt at nonchalance:

"You – you don't see anyone on the lawn, William, do you?"

Again William looked straight at Miss Moyna Greene.

"No," he said innocently. "There ain't no one there."

Miss Moyna Greene disappeared through the drawing-room window.

"All the bad luck," repeated William artlessly, "s'posed to come *from* the one they're with when they see it, but I don' b'lieve anyone ever *has* seen it if you ask me."

He looked up at Mr Cranthorpe-Cranborough. Mr Cranthorpe-Cranborough was still yellow and still perspiring. He took out his handkerchief and mopped his brow.

"You don' look very well," said William kindly, "can I do anythin' for you?"

Mr Cranthorpe-Cranborough brought his eyes with an effort from the direction in which Miss Moyna Greene had vanished to William. And his expression changed. He seemed to realise for the first time the full import of his vision.

"Yes, William," he said with fear and shrinking in his

manner. "You can – er – you can fetch me a railway time-table, my dear boy, if you'll be so good."

William and Ethel and Robert had gone to bed.

Mr and Mrs Brown sat in the drawing-room alone.

"He went very suddenly, didn't he?" said Mr Brown, "I thought I'd find him here tonight."

"I can't understand it," said Mrs Brown, "he behaved most *strangely*. *Suddenly* came in and said he was going. Gave no reason and was most *peculiar* in his manner."

"And you didn't arrange anything about William going there?"

"I tried to. I said should we consider it settled, but he said he was afraid he'd have no room for William, after all. I suggested putting him on a waiting list, but he said he'd no room on his waiting list either. He wouldn't even stay to discuss it. He went off to the station at once though I told him he'd have to wait half an hour for a train. And the last thing he said was that he was sorry but he'd *no* room for William. He said it several times. So strange after his offering to take him at a special price."

"Very strange," said Mr Brown slowly. "He was – all right at lunch you say?"

"Quite. He was talking then as if William were going."

"And what did he do after lunch?"

"He went into the garden to rest."

"And who was with him?"

"No one . . . Oh, except William for a few minutes."

"Ah," said Mr Brown, and remembered the sphinx-like look upon William's face when he said Good-night to him. "I'd give a good deal to have been present at those few minutes – but the secret, whatever it was, will die with William, I suppose. William possesses the supreme gift of being able to keep his own counsel."

"Are you sorry, dear, that William's not going to a boarding-school?"

"I don't think I am," said Mr Brown.

"I should have thought you'd have found it so nice and quiet without him."

"Doubtless I should. But it would also have been extremely dull."

CHAPTER TWO

WILLIAM HOLDS THE STAGE

IT WAS AN old boy of William's school, called Mr Welbecker, who with well-intentioned but mistaken enthusiasm offered a prize to the form that should act a scene from Shakespeare most successfully. The old boy in question had written an article on Shakespeare which had appeared in the columns of the local press, and, being a man of more means than discernment, thought it well to commemorate his intellectual achievement and immortalise his name by instituting the Welbecker Shakespeare Acting Shield in his old school.

The headmaster and the staff received his offer with conventional gratitude but without enthusiasm. Several of the senior members of the staff were heard to express a wish that that fool Welbecker could have the trouble of organising the thing himself, adding that he jolly well wouldn't do it more than once. The junior staff expressed all this more simply and forcibly by saying that the blighter ought to be hanged. To make matters worse, the blighter arrived at the school one morning, unheralded and unexpected, armed with innumerable copies of his article on Shakespeare, privately printed and bound in white vellum with gold lettering, and, after distributing them broadcast, offered to give a lecture on Shakespeare to the school. The headmaster hastily said that it was impossible to arrange for him to give a lecture to the school. He said politely and unblushingly that he was sure that it would be a deep disappointment to the boys, but that the routine of the school would not allow of it on that particular day. The author offered to come another time when arrangements could be made beforehand. The headmaster replied evasively that he would see about it.

It was at this moment that the second master came in to ask what was to be done about IIIa, explaining that the master who should be teaching it had suddenly been taken ill. He implied in discreet, well-chosen words that IIIa was engaged in raising Cain in their form room and that no one within a mile of them could hear himself speak. The headmaster raised a hand to his head wearily, then his eye fell upon the Shakespearean author, and he brightened.

"Perhaps you'd give your lecture on Shakespeare to IIIa," he suggested suavely.

"It's young Brown and that set," murmured the second master warningly. The headmaster's expression brightened still further. So might a man look who was sending his bitterest enemy unarmed and unsuspecting into a lions' den.

"Splendid!" he said heartily, "splendid! I'm sure they'll find your lecture most interesting, Welbecker. *Good* morning. I hope to see you, of course, before you go."

A sudden silence – a silence of interest and surprise – greeted the entry of Mr Welbecker into the classroom of IIIa.

"Now boys," he said breezily, "I want to give you a little talk about Shakespeare, and I want you to ask me questions freely, because I'm – er – well, I'm what you might call an expert on the subject. I've written a little book, some copies of which I have with me now, and which I'm going to give to the boys who seem to me to show the most intelligence. I'm sure that they will always be among your greatest treasures, because – well, it isn't *everyone* who can write a book, you know, is it?"

"I've written a book," put in William nonchalantly.

"Perhaps," said Mr Welbecker, smiling tolerantly, "but you've not had it published, have you?"

"No," said William, "I've not tried to have it published yet."

"And it wasn't on Shakespeare, was it?" said Mr Welbecker, smiling still more tolerantly.

"No," said William. "It was about someone a jolly sight more int'restin' than Shakespeare. It was about a pirate called Dick of the Bloody Hand, an' he started off in search of adventure an' he came to—"

"Yes," said Mr Welbecker hastily, "but I just want to tell you a little about Shakespeare first. Now the theory I incline to is that Bacon wrote the plays of Shakespeare."

"I wrote a play once," said William, "and people acted it, but they all forgot their parts, so it didn't come to much, but it was a jolly fine play all the same."

"I wish you wouldn't keep interrupting," said Mr Welbecker testily.

"I thought you said we could ask questions," said William.

"Yes, I did, but you're not asking questions."

"I know I'm not," said William, "but I don't see any

difference in asking a question and telling you something int'restin'."

Most of the class had by now settled down to their own devices – quiet or otherwise. William was the only one who seemed to be taking any interest in the lecture or the lecturer. William, on the strength of his play and story, considered himself a literary character, and was quite willing to give a hearing to a brother artist.

"Well," said Mr Welbecker, assuming his lecturer's manner, gazing round at his audience, and returning at last reluctantly to William, "I repeat that I incline to the theory that the plays of Shakespeare were written by Bacon."

"How could they be?" said William.

"I've already said that I wished you wouldn't keep interrupting," snapped the lecturer.

"That *was* a question," said William triumphantly. "You can't say that wasn't a question, and you said we could ask questions. How could that other man Ham—"

"I said Bacon."

"Well, it's nearly the same," said William. "Well, how could this man Bacon write them if Shakespeare wrote them?"

"Ah, but you see I don't believe that Shakespeare did write them," said Mr Welbecker mysteriously.

"Well, why's he got his name printed on all the books then?" said William. "He must've told the printers he did, or they wouldn't put his name on, an' he ought to know. An' if this other man Eggs—"

"I said Bacon," snapped Mr Welbecker again.

"Well, Bacon, then," said William, "well, if this man Bacon wrote them, they wouldn't put this man Shake-

28

"YOU SAID WE COULD ASK QUESTIONS," SAID WILLIAM.

speare's name on the books. They wouldn't be allowed
to. They'd get put in prison for it. The only way he could
have done it was by poisoning this man Shakespeare and
then stealing his plays. That's what I'd have done, anyway,
if I'd been him, and I'd wanted to say I'd written them."

"That's all nonsense," said Mr Welbecker sharply. "Of
course I'm willing to admit that it's an open question."
Then, returning to his breezy manner and making an
unsuccessful attempt to enlarge his audience: "Now, boys,
I want you all please to listen to me—"

No one responded. Those who were playing noughts
and crosses continued to play noughts and crosses. Those
who were engaged in mimic battles, the ammunition of
which consisted in pellets of blotting-paper soaked in ink,

continued to be so engaged. Those who were playing that game of cricket in which a rubber represents the ball and a ruler the bat remained engrossed in it. The boy who was drawing low-pitched but irritating sounds from a whistle continued to draw low-pitched but irritating sounds from a whistle. Dejectedly Mr Welbecker returned to his sole auditor.

"I want first to tell you the story of the play of which you are all going to act a scene for the shield that I am presenting," he said. "There was a man called Hamlet—"

"You just said he was called Bacon," said William.

"I did *not* say he was called Bacon," snapped Mr Welbecker.

"Yes, 'scuse me, you did," said William politely. "When I called him Ham you said it was Bacon, and now you're calling him Ham yourself."

"This was a different man," said Mr Welbecker. "*Listen!* This man was called Hamlet and his uncle had killed his father because he wanted to marry his mother."

"What did he want to marry his mother for?" said William. "I've never heard of anyone wanting to marry their mother."

"It was *Hamlet's* mother he wanted to marry."

"Oh, that man that you think wrote the plays."

"No, that was Bacon."

"You said it was Ham a minute ago. Whenever I say it's Bacon you say it's Ham, and whenever I say it's Ham you say it's Bacon. I don't think you know *which* his name was."

"Will you *listen*!" said the distraught lecturer. "This man Hamlet decided to kill his uncle."

"Why?"

"I've told you. Because his uncle had killed his father."

"Whose father?"

"*Hamlet's*. There's a beautiful girl in the play called Ophelia, and Hamlet had once wanted to marry her."

"You just said he wanted to marry his mother."

"I did *not*. I wish you'd listen. Then he went mad, and this girl fell into the river. It was supposed to be an accident, but probably—"

"He pushed her in," supplied William.

"*Who* pushed her?" demanded Mr Welbecker irritably.

"I thought you were going to say that that man Bacon pushed her in."

"*Hamlet*, you mean."

"I tell you what," said William confidingly, "let's say Eggs for both of them. Then we shan't get so muddled. Eggs means whichever of them it was."

"Rubbish!" exploded the lecturer. "Listen – I'll begin all over again." But just at that minute the bell rang, and the headmaster entered the room. Immediately whistle, rubbers, rulers, noughts and crosses, pellets, vanished as by magic, and twenty-five earnest, attentive faces were turned towards the lecturer. So intent were they on the lecture that apparently they were unaware that the headmaster had entered the room, for not one turned in his direction.

"This is the end of the period, Welbecker," said the headmaster. "A thousand thanks for your help and your most interesting lecture. I'm sure you've enjoyed it tremendously, haven't you boys?"

A thunder of applause bore tribute to their enjoyment.

"Now," continued the headmaster rather maliciously, "I want one of you to give me a short account of Mr Welbecker's lecture. Let any one of you who thinks he can do so put up his hand."

Only one hand went up, and it was William's.

"Well, Brown?" said the headmaster.

"Please, sir, he told us that he thinks that the plays of Shakespeare were really written by a man called Ham and that Shakespeare poisoned this man called Ham and stole the plays and then pretended he'd written them. And then a man called Bacon pushed a woman into a pond because he wanted to marry his mother. And there's a man called Eggs, but I've forgotten what he did except that—"

Mr Welbecker's complexion had assumed a greenish hue.

"That will do, Brown," said the headmaster very quietly.

Despite this contretemps, the preparations for the Shakespeare acting competition continued apace. Mr Welbecker had chosen Act III, Scene I, to be acted for the Shield. The parts of the Queen and Ophelia were to be played by boys, "as was the custom in Shakespeare's time," said Mr Welbecker, who seemed to cherish a pathetic delusion that no one had ever known anything about Shakespeare before his article appeared in the local press.

"I'm not going to be the woman that gets pushed into a pond," said William firmly. "I don't mind being the one that pushes her, and I don't mind being the one called Ham that poisons Shakespeare. I don't much mind which of them I am so long as I'm not the one that gets pushed into a pond, and as long as I've got a lot to say. When I'm in a play I like to have a lot to say."

His interest in the play was increased by the fact that Dorinda Lane was once more staying at her aunt's in the village. Dorinda was a little girl with dark hair and dimples, who was the temporary possessor of William's heart, a hard-boiled organ that generally scorned thraldom to any woman. Dorinda, however, appeared on his horizon so seldom that, for the short duration of her visits, he could stoop from his heroic pinnacle of manliness to admire her without losing prestige in his own eyes.

"I'm goin' to be in a play at school," he informed her the morning after Mr Welbecker's lecture.

She gave a little cry of excitement. Her admiration of William was absolute and unmixed.

"Oh, William!" she said, "how lovely! What are you going to be?"

"I'm not quite sure," said William, "but anyway I'm goin' to be the most important person in it."

"Oh, *are* you, William?"

"Yes. I'm going to be the one that poisons Bacon or that pushes Ham into a pond or something like that. Anyway, we had a lecture about it, and I was the only one that knew anything about it at the end, so they're going to give me the biggest part."

"Oh, William, how lovely! Have they told you so?"

William hesitated.

"Well, they've as good as told me," he said. "I mean, I was the only one that knew anything about it when

"I'M GOING TO BE THE MOST IMPORTANT PERSON IN THE PLAY,"
SAID WILLIAM.

they'd finished giving this lecture, so they're sure to give
me the biggest part. In fact" – finally surrendering to his
imagination – "in fact, they *told* me they were. They said:
'You seem to be the only one that knows anything about
this man Eggs what wrote the play so you choose what
you'd like to be in it.' "

34

"Oh, William," said Dorinda, "I think you're wonderful."

After this William, convinced by his own eloquence, firmly believed that he was to be offered the best part in the scene, because of his masterly recapitulation of its plot. In order to be sure of making a good choice, he borrowed a Shakespeare from his father, turned to the scene (with much difficulty), and began to read it through. He found it as incomprehensible as if it had been written in a foreign language, but he was greatly struck by the speech beginning "To be or not to be—" It was long, it was even more incomprehensible than the rest of the scene, it went with a weirdly impressive swing. William loved speeches that were long and incomprehensible and that went with a swing. He mouthed it with infinite gusto and many gesticulations, striding to and fro in his bedroom. He decided quite finally that he would be Hamlet.

His surprise and disgust, therefore, were unbounded when his form master told him that he was to be one of the attendants on the king, and that, as such, he would not be required to say anything at all.

"You just go in first of all and stand by the throne and then go out when the king goes out."

"But I want to say something," protested William.

"I've no doubt you do," said his form master dryly. "I've never known you yet when you didn't. But as it happens, the attendant doesn't speak. By a strange oversight Shakespeare didn't write any lines for him."

"Well, I don't mind writin' some myself. I'll write it and learn it."

"If you learn it as well as you learnt your Latin verbs

35

yesterday," said the form master sarcastically, "it'll be worth listening to."

"Well, I don't *like* Latin verbs," said William, "and I *do* like acting."

But it was in vain. His form master was adamant. He was to be one of the king's attendants and he was not to say anything. William's first plan was to feign illness on the day of the play and to tell Dorinda that a substitute had had to be hastily found for him but that he would have done the part much better. There were, however, obvious drawbacks to this course. For one thing he had never yet managed to feign illness with any success. His family doctor was a suspicious and, in William's eyes, inhuman being, who always drove William from his sick-bed to whatever he was trying to avoid by draughts of nauseous medicine. ("It's better than bein' poisoned anyway," William would say bitterly, as he finally abandoned his symptoms.) Moreover, even if he succeeded in outwitting the doctor (a thing he had never done yet) the whole proceeding would be rather tame. If there was anything going on William liked to be in it.

It was a chance remark of his father's that sent a ray of light into the gloom of the situation.

It happened that this same play was being acted at a London theatre, and that the actor who should have played Hamlet had been taken ill and the part played by another member of the cast at the last minute.

"This other fellow knew the part," said his father, "so he stepped into the breach."

"Why did he do that?" said William.

"Do what?" asked his father.

"Step into that thing you said."

"What thing?"

"You just said he stepped into something."

"I said he played the part."

"Well, you said he stepped into somethin', an' I thought perhaps he broke it like Robert did steppin' into one of the footlights when he was acting in that play the football club did."

His father's only reply was a grunt that was obviously intended to close the conversation.

But William's way now lay clear before him. He would learn Hamlet's part, and on the night of the play, when Hamlet was taken ill, he would come forward to play the part for him. ("An' I won't go messin' about steppin' into things same as the one in London did," he said sternly.)

In William's eyes the part of Hamlet consisted solely of the "To be or not to be" speech. "If I learn that I'll be all right," he told himself. "I can jus' make up the rest. Jus' say what comes into my head when they say things to me."

Every night he repeated the speech before his looking-glass with eloquent and windmill-like gestures that swept everything off his dressing-table onto the floor in all directions.

As his head was the only part of his person that was visible in the looking-glass, he did not trouble to dress up more than his head for his part. Sometimes he clothed it Arab fashion in his towel, sometimes in his Red Indian head-dress, sometimes in his father's top hat, "borrowed" for the occasion. On the whole he thought that the top hat gave the best effect.

"Are you *really* going to be the hero, William?" said Dorinda when next she met him.

"Yes, I have a speech that takes hours and hours to say. The longest there's ever been in a play. I stand in the middle of the stage, and I go on talkin' an' talkin' sayin' the things in this speech with no one stoppin' me, or interruptin' me. For *hours*. 'Cause I'm the person the whole play's written about."

"Oh, William, how lovely! What's the speech about?"

As William, though now able to repeat the speech almost perfectly, had not the faintest idea what it was about, he merely smiled mysteriously and said: "Oh, you'll have to wait and see."

"Is it funny, William? Will it make me laugh? I *love* funny things."

William considered. For all he knew the speech might be intended to be humorous. On the other hand, of course, it might not be. Having no key to its meaning, he could not tell.

"You'll have to wait and see," he said with the air of one to whom weighty state secrets are entrusted, and who is bound on honour not to betray them.

He had now abandoned his looking-glass as an audience, and strode to and fro uttering his speech with its ample accompaniment of gestures to an audience of his wash-stand and a chair and a photograph of his mother's and father's wedding group that had slowly descended the ladder of importance, working its way in the course of the years from the drawing-room to the dining-room, from the dining-room to the morning-room, from the morning-room to the hall, from the hall to the staircase, and then through his mother's, Robert's, and Ethel's bedrooms to the bottom rung of the ladder in William's.

William, of course, did not see the wash-stand and the chair and the wedding group; he saw ranks upon serried ranks of intent faces, Dorinda's standing out from among them with startling clearness.

"To be or not to be," he would declaim, "that is the question, whether 'tis nobler in the slings to suffer
The mind and arrows of opposing fortune
Or to die to sleep against a sea of troubles.
And by opposing end there."

Even William did not pretend to get every word in its exact place. As he said to himself: "It's as sens'ble as what's in the book, anyway, and it sounds all right."

The subordinate part that he took in the rehearsals as the king's attendant did not trouble him in the least. He was not the king's attendant. He was Hamlet. He was the tall, dark boy called Dalrymple (he had adenoids and a slight lisp but excellent memory) who played Hamlet. It was he, William, not Dalrymple, who repeated that long and thrilling speech to an enthralled audience. So entirely did William trust in his star that he had not the slightest doubt that Dalrymple would develop some illness on the day of the play. William's mother had an enormous book with the title "Every-day Ailments." William glanced through it idly and was much cheered by it. There were so many illnesses that it seemed impossible that Dalrymple – a mere mortal and susceptible to all the germs with which the air was apparently laden – should not be stricken down by one or another of them on the day of the play. Dorinda met him in the village the day before the performance.

"I'm *longing* for tomorrow, William," she said.

And William, without the slightest qualm of doubt, replied:

"Oh, yes, it'll be jolly fine. You look out for my long speech."

The day of the performance dawned. No news of any sudden illness of Dalrymple's reached William, yet he still felt no doubts. His star had marked him out for Hamlet, and Hamlet he would be. His mother, who was anxious for him not to be late, saw him off for the performance at what William considered an unduly early hour with many admonitions not to loiter on the way. She herself was coming later as part of the audience. William had a strong dislike of arriving too early at any objective. He considered that his mother had made him set off quite a quarter of an hour too soon, and therefore that he had a quarter of an hour to spend on the way. He still felt no doubts that he would play the part of Hamlet, but he was not narrow in his interests, and he realised even at that moment that there were other things in the world than Hamlet. There was the stream in Crown Woods (he had decided to go the longer way through Crown Woods in order to make up the quarter of an hour), there was a hedge sparrow's nest, there was a curious insect which William had never seen before and of which he thought that he must be the first discoverer, there was a path that William had not noticed on his previous visits to the wood and that had therefore to be explored, there was a tree whose challenge to climb it William could not possibly resist. Even William realised, on emerging from the wood, that he had spent in it more than the quarter of an hour that he considered his due.

He ran in the direction of the school. An excited

group of people was standing at the gate, looking out for him. They received him with a stream of indignant reproaches, bundled him into his form room and began to pull off his clothes and hustle him into his attendant's uniform. ("It's time to *begin*. We've been waiting for you for *ages*. Why on *earth* couldn't you get here in time?") All the others had changed and were ready in their costumes. Hamlet looked picturesque in black velvet slashed with purple, wearing a silver chain. William tried to collect his forces, but his legs were being thrust into tights by one person, his hair was being mercilessly brushed by another, and his face was being made up by another. Whenever he opened his mouth to speak, it received a stick of make-up or an eyebrow pencil or a hare's foot.

"Now don't forget," said the form master, who was also the producer, "you go on first of all and stand by the throne. Stand quite stiffly, as I showed you, and in a few moments the king and the others will come on."

And William, his faculties still in a whirl, was thrust unceremoniously upon the empty stage.

He stood there facing a sea of upturned, intent faces. Among them in the second row he discerned that of Dorinda, her eyes fixed expectantly upon him.

Instinctively and without a moment's hesitation, he stepped forward and with a sweeping gesture launched into his speech:

"To be or not to be that is the question

Whether 'tis nobler in the mind to suffer—"

"Come off, you young fool," hissed the form master wildly from behind the scenes.

But William had got well into his stride and was not coming off for anyone.

41

"The stings and arrows of outrageous fortune." (For a wonder he was getting the words in their right places.)

"Or to take arms against a sea of troubles."

The best thing, of course, would have been to lower the curtain, but there was no curtain to lower.

"COME *OFF*, I TELL YOU," REPEATED THE FORM MASTER FRANTICALLY.

Screens had been set along the edge of the stage and had been folded up when the performance was to begin.

"Come *off*, I tell you," repeated the form master frantically.

"And by opposing end there. To sleep to die."

William had forgotten everything in the world but himself, his words, and Dorinda. He was unaware of the

WILLIAM WAS UNAWARE OF THE FROZEN FACES OF THE
HEADMASTER AND OF MR WELBECKER, WHO SAT IN THE FRONT
ROW.

crowd of distraught players hissing and gesticulating off the stage; he was unaware of his form master's frenzied commands, of the frozen faces of the headmaster and Mr Welbecker, who sat holding his shield ready for presentation in the front row.

"No more and by a sleep to say an end."

The form master decided to act. The boy had evidently gone mad. The only thing to do was to go boldly on to the stage and drag him off. This the form master attempted to do. He stalked on to the stage and put out his hand to seize William. William, vaguely aware that someone was trying to stop him saying his speech, reacted promptly, and dodged to the other side of the stage, still continuing his recital.

"The thousand natural shocks the flesh and hair is."

The form master, whose blood was now up, plunged across the stage. Once more William dodged his outstretched hand, and, still breathlessly reciting, reached the other end of the stage again. Then followed the diverting spectacle of the form master chasing William round the stage – William dodging, doubling, and all the time continuing his speech. Someone had the timely idea of trying to set up the screens again, but it was a manoeuvre that defeated its own ends, for William (still reciting) merely dodged round and behind them and unfortunately one of them fell down on the top of the form master. A mighty roar ascended from the audience. Dorinda was rocking to and fro with mirth and clapping with all her might and main. The unseemly performance came to an end at last. The players joined the form master in the chase, and William, still reciting, was dragged ingloriously from the stage.

Mr Welbecker turned a purple face to the headmaster.

"This is an outrage," he said; "an insult. I should not dream of presenting my shield to a school in which I have seen this exhibition."

"I agree that it's a most regrettable incident, Welbecker," said the headmaster suavely, "and I think that in the circumstances your decision is amply justified."

Dorinda was wiping tears of laughter from her eyes.

"Wasn't William *wonderful*?" she said.

It was, of course, felt by the staff of William's school that someone ought to deal drastically with William, but it was so difficult not to regard him as a public benefactor (for the thought of the annual Welbecker Shield Shakespeare Competition had begun to assume the proportion of a nightmare in the minds of an already overworked staff) that no definite move had been taken in the matter beyond the rough and (very) ready primitive measures meted out on the spot by the form master.

School had broken up the next day, and, when it had quite safely broken up, the headmaster and form master informed each other just for the look of the thing that each thought the other was dealing officially with William.

"It was unpardonable," said the headmaster, "but it's too late to do anything now that the term's over. I'll send for him at the beginning of next term."

"That will be best," said the form master, who was quite sure that he would forget.

Mrs Brown had crept out of the hall at the beginning of the incident and was pretending to herself and everyone else that she had not gone to the performance at all, and so knew nothing about it.

A fortnight after the end of term William went to tea with Dorinda – a magnificent cross-country journey involving a train ride and two 'bus rides. Dorinda's mother supplied a sumptuous tea, and William, watched admiringly by Dorinda, did full justice to it.

"Dorinda so much enjoyed that play at your school, William," said Dorinda's mother, watching the rapid disappearance of an iced cake with dispassionate wonder. "She said when she came home that she never laughed so much in all her life. She couldn't remember much of the plot but she said it was awfully funny. It was a farce, wasn't it?"

"Yes," said William, unwilling to admit that he did not know what the word farce meant.

"What was it called? We used to act a lot of farces when I was young."

William gazed frowningly into the distance.

"I've forgotten," he said, then his face cleared. "Oh yes, I remember. It was called 'Eggs and Bacon'."

CHAPTER THREE

WILLIAM AND THE CHINESE GOD

M R MARKSON, the headmaster of William's school, was very large and very red-faced and very loud-voiced and very irascible. Behind this mask of terror Mr Markson was in reality a rather shy and very well-meaning man. He liked big boys and got on well with them. He disliked small boys and glared at them and roared at them on principle.

William and his friends came in contact with this ogre seldom, and on occasions of decided unpleasantness.

In their eyes he was all the fabulous masters of antiquity and all the ogres of fairyland rolled into one. They trembled beneath his rolling eye and booming voice. Which was just as well, because these were about the only things beneath which they did tremble.

They were discussing this grim potentate on their way home from school.

"He's the nasty temperedest man in the world," said Ginger solemnly. "I know he is. I know there's not another man as nasty tempered as what he is in all the world."

"He swished Rawlings for jus' walkin' through the stream in the playground," contributed Henry, "an'

Rawlings is short-sighted, you know. An' he said he din't *see* the stream till he'd got right over it, but ole Markie swished him jus' the same."

"When he jus' *looks* at me," admitted Ginger, "it makes me feel kinder queer."

"Yes, an' when he *yells* like what he does," said Douglas, "it makes me jump like – like—"

"Like a frog," suggested Ginger helpfully.

"Frog yourself!"

"I din' mean you *was* a frog," explained Ginger. "I only meant you jumped like a frog."

"Well, I don't jump like a frog more'n other people do," said Douglas pugnaciously.

"Oh, shut up arguing," said Henry, who had been enjoying the collective indictment of "Old Markie," and did not wish it to tail off into a combat between Douglas and Ginger. "I guess," he went on darkly, "that if some people knew what he was like really an' – an' the way he shouts an' swishes people an' – an' carries on, I guess he'd be put in prison or hung or something. There's laws," he added vaguely, "to stop people goin' on at other people the way he does."

William had listened to this conversation in silence. William disliked belonging to the majority of the terrorised. He preferred always to belong to the minority of the terror-inspiring, or at least of the intrepid. He gave a short, scornful laugh.

"I'm not frightened of him," he said with a swagger.

They gazed at him, aghast at this patent untruth.

"Oh, *aren't* you?" said Ginger meaningly.

"No, *an'* I'm not," retorted William. "I wun't mind sayin' anythin' to him, I wun't. I wun't mind – I wun't

48

mind jus' tellin' him what I thought of him any time, I wun't."

"Oh, *wun't* you?" said Ginger disagreeably, piqued by this unexpected attitude of William's. "Oh, no," sarcastically, "you're not frightened of him, *you* aren't. *You* wasn't frightened of him las' Tuesday, was you?"

William was momentarily disconcerted by this reference to an occasion when he had incurred the public wrath of the monster for scuffling in prayers, and had been summoned to his study afterwards. But only momentarily.

"P'raps you *thought* I was," he conceded in a tone of kindly indulgence. "I daresay you *thought* I was. I daresay you judge eve'body by yourself an' *thought* I was."

"Well, you *looked* frightened," said Henry.

"An' you *sounded* frightened," said Ginger, and mimicked "Yes, sir . . . No, sir . . . please I didn't mean to, sir."

William looked at them with an air of superior pity.

"Yes, I daresay you *thought* I was frightened," he said, and added darkly, "you see you din't hear what I said to him in his study afterwards. I guess," he added with a short meaning laugh, "he'll leave *me* alone after that."

The others were dumbfounded by this attitude. For a minute the sheer impudence of it deprived them of the power of speech. Ginger recovered first.

"All right," he said, "we're jus' at his house now. All right, if you're not frightened of him, go in. Jus' go an' ring at the door an' tell him you're not frightened of him."

"He knows," said William simply.

But they were closing him in around the gate, preventing his further progress down the road.

"Well, go in an' tell him again," said Douglas, "case he's forgot."

William, at bay, looked up at Mr Markson's house, inappropriately termed The Nest. He wished that he had not made his gesture of defiance in its immediate vicinity. Then a cheering thought occurred to him.

"An' I would, too," he said, striking a heroic attitude. "An' I would'f he was at home. But he's at school. He's at school till six o'clock today."

"All right, go an' walk into his house an' take somethin' jus' to *show* you aren't frightened of him," said Ginger.

"That'd be stealin'," said William piously.

"You could take it back afterwards," said Douglas. "You aren't fright'ned of him, so it'd be all right."

"No, I'm not goin' to," said William.

Henry crowed triumphantly.

"You're fright'ned of him," they jeered.

Suddenly William's blood was up. When William's blood was up things happened.

"All right," he said. "I'll – I'll *show* you."

Without waiting to consider his decision in the calm light of reason he went boldly up to the front door. There his courage began to fail. He knew that no power on earth would nerve his arm to knock on the ogre's dreaded front door. But there was a drawing-room to the right of the door. One of the French windows leading from this drawing-room on to the drive was open.

The drawing-room seemed to be empty. Steeling his heart and spurring his flickering courage by the thought of his jeering friends without, William plunged into the room, seized the first thing he saw, plunged out, and with a beating heart and unsteady knees ran down the drive to join the little crowd of boys gaping through the gate of The Nest.

His panic left him as he neared safety and his swagger returned. He held out his booty on one hand. It was a small and (though William did not know it) very valuable Chinese figure of a god.

"There!" he said. "I've been in his drawing-room and fetched that."

They gazed at him speechless. William had once again consolidated his position as leader.

"Sorter pot thing out of his drawin'-room," he explained carelessly. "D'you think I'm afraid of him *now*?" he ended with a short derisive laugh.

Henry found his voice. "Well, you've gotter put it back now," he said, "an' – an' p'raps that won't be's easy's takin' it."

"'F you think it was *easy* takin' it—" began William indignantly.

But at that moment a tall figure – ferocious-looking even in the distance – appeared at the end of the lane.

William had been wrong. Mr Markson was not staying at school till six.

By the time Mr Markson reached the gate of The Nest, William and his friends were mere specks on the horizon.

In the safe refuge of his bedroom William took the Chinese figure out of his pocket and looked at it distastefully. He didn't know how to get the beastly thing back, and he was sure there'd be a fuss if he didn't get the beastly thing back, and he wished he'd never taken the beastly thing, and he blamed Douglas and Ginger and Henry for the whole affair.

If only they'd taken his word that he wasn't frightened of old Markie, instead of making him go in and get the beastly thing – and ten to one old Markie would catch him as he was putting it back and – and – and there'd be a *norful* fuss.

He considered the advisability of giving it a temporary hiding place in one of his drawers among his handkerchiefs or shirts or collars, then dismissed the idea. His mother might find it and demand explanations. On the whole, his pocket was the safest place for the present.

He went downstairs feeling gloomy and disillusioned. All the people one read about in books – Odysseus and Tarzan and the rest of them – could do anything they liked and nothing ever happened to them, while he couldn't even say he wasn't fright'ned of old Markie without getting a beastly little pot thing shoved on to him, that there'd be an awful fuss about if anyone found out he'd got it.

He wandered downstairs, his mind still occupied with the problem of returning the china image before Mr Markson had discovered its absence. Suppose someone had seen him go in and fetch it and told old Markie, and old Markie summoned him into his study tomorrow morning after prayers. William turned hot and cold at the thought. That gesture of defiance and courage had been very effective and enjoyable at the time, but its consequences might be unpleasant.

"What's the matter, darling?" inquired Mrs Brown solicitously as William entered the drawing-room.

"Why?" said William guiltily, afraid that in some way his appearance betrayed his late escapade.

"You look so sad," said his mother fondly.

William emitted his famous laugh – short and bitter.

"Huh!" he ejaculated. "I bet *you'd* be sad if—"

He decided on second thoughts not to make any detailed explanation and stopped short.

"If what, dear?" said Mrs Brown sympathetically.

"If you'd got all the troubles what I've got," said William darkly.

"Yes, but what sort of troubles, dear?" said Mrs Brown.

"Oh, people botherin' you an' not b'lievin' what you say an' – an' gettin' things you don't want shoved on to you," said William gloomily.

At this point he caught sight of his reflection in a full-length mirror on the wall and was greatly disconcerted to discover that the Chinese figure made a bulge in his pocket that seemed to call aloud for comment. At any minute his mother might demand to know what it was. He took advantage of her turning to the window to transfer the figure from his pocket to a small table by the wall just where he stood. He put it well at the back of a lot of other ornaments. Surely no one would notice it there. It could surely stay there quite safely till the coast was clear for taking it back, anyway.

He heaved a deep sigh and passed a hand over his brow. Life was very wearing – and there'd certainly be a most awful fuss if anyone found out – an' all Henry's and Ginger's and Douglas's fault – it ought to be a lesson to them to believe what people said in the future. Anyway

– he found great comfort in the thought – he'd *shown* 'em.

He joined his mother at the window, scowling gloomily. Suddenly his gloomy scowl changed to a look of rigid horror. Mr Markson was coming along the road with Ethel ... now they were turning in at the gate of William's house. And there on a table in the drawing-room, which presumably they would soon enter, reposed Mr Markson's Chinese image. William had had many nightmares in his time but none as bad as this.

Ethel, although William's sister, was admittedly the prettiest girl for miles around, and Mr Markson, although William's headmaster, was beneath his mask of ferocity quite a simple-hearted man, who liked pretty girls and had been much attracted by Ethel when introduced to her the week before.

They entered the room almost immediately, followed by two old ladies who were friends of Mrs Brown. Mr Markson took no notice of William. He knew, of course, that there was a small boy in the room who might or might not be a pupil at his school, but out of school hours Mr Markson ignored all small boys on principle.

To William suddenly the Chinese image on the little table seemed to dominate the room. It seemed to tower above every other object, not excluding the grandfather clock. It seemed to yell aloud to its owner: "Hi, you! I'm here! I'm here! I'm here! I'm here!"

Instinctively William stepped in front of the table, placing his small but solid person between the now hateful image and its rightful owner. Standing thus, red-faced with apprehension and determination, he glared fiercely around the room as though daring anyone to attempt to dislodge him. There was a How-Horatius-kept-the-Bridge air about him.

Ethel and Mr Markson and Mrs Brown and one of the old ladies sat at the other end of the room and began to discuss animatedly a forthcoming village pageant. The other old lady drifted across to William and sat down on a chair near him. She pointed kindly to another chair near her.

"Sit down, little boy," she said, "pray don't stand, though it's nice to see a little boy so polite nowadays."

William's scowl deepened.

"I'd rather stand, thanks," he said.

But the old lady persisted.

"No, do sit down," she said with a pleasant smile. "I want to have a nice long talk with you; I'm so fond of little boys. But you must sit down or I shan't feel comfortable."

William was disconcerted for a minute, then he recovered his aplomb.

"I – I can't sit down," he said mysteriously.

The lady gaped at him, amazed.

"Why, dear?" she said sympathetically.

"I've hurt my legs," said William with a flash of inspiration. "I can't bend my knees. Not for sitting down. I *gotta* stand."

He scowled at her more ferociously than ever as he spoke.

"My poor little boy," said the old lady sympathetically. "I'm *so* sorry. Do you have to stand up all the time? What do the doctors say?"

"They say – they say jus' that," said William lamely, "that I've gotta stand up all the time."

"I'VE HURT MY LEGS," SAID WILLIAM, WITH A FLASH OF
INSPIRATION. "I CAN'T BEND MY KNEES."

"But there's – hope of your being cured, I suppose,
dear?" said the old lady anxiously.

"Oh, yes," William reassured her.

"*When* do they say you'll be all right?" went on the
lady earnestly.

"Oh, any time after today," said William unthinkingly.

"You can *lie* down, I suppose?" said the old lady, evidently much distressed by William's mysterious complaint.

"Oh yes," said William, who by this time had almost convinced himself of the reality of his disease. "I can go to bed at night and that sort of thing."

"Well, dear, won't you come and lie down now?" said the old lady. "We'll go over to the window and you can lie down on the sofa and I'll sit on the chair near, and we'll have a nice little talk. It's so nice over there in the sunshine."

William moistened his lips.

"I – I think I won't move, thank you," said William.

"But you can walk, dear, can't you?"

"Oh, yes, I can walk, but—" he stopped and gazed around, seeking inspiration from the wallpaper and ceiling.

"It's so nice and light over there," coaxed the old lady.

Inspiration came again with a flash. William's face cleared.

"I'm not s'posed to be in the light," he said brightly, "because I've got bad eyes."

The old lady gazed at him weakly.

"Bad – bad eyes, did you say?"

"Yes," said William pleasantly, relieved to have found another plausible excuse for not relinquishing his post. "I can't stand the light," he explained earnestly. "I've gotta stay in dark places 'cause of my eyes."

"B-but how terrible," said the old lady, horrified to the depth of her kindly old soul. "Bad legs and bad— It's almost incredible." She gazed in silence at his stolid and almost crudely healthy countenance, while a dim

57

suspicion crept into her mind that it was, indeed, incredible. "Can't sit down or bend your knees?" she repeated in amazement.

"No," said William unblushingly.

"And can't bear the light on your eyes?"

"No," said William, staring at her unblinkingly. "Bad eyes."

Well, of course, thought the nice old lady, it might be true. One did hear of sad cases of terrible illnesses among quite young children.

She crossed over to the other group.

"I'm so sorry to hear of your poor little boy's ill-health, Mrs Brown," she said.

There was a moment's tense silence, during which the members of the other group stared open-mouthed from the nice old lady to the robustly healthy William, from the robustly healthy William back to the nice old lady. The silence was broken by William who, realising the moment was one that called for discretion rather than valour, fled from the room with the speed of an arrow from a bow.

Mrs Brown's bewildered demand for an explanation was lost in a sudden exclamation of astonishment from Mr Markson, who was staring in amazement at the little table of ornaments that William's flight had revealed.

"Er – excuse me," he said and going across the room picked up the little Chinese ornament. "Most extraordinary," he said, "I have an exact replica of this at home and I was assured that it was absolutely unique. May I ask without impertinence, Mrs Brown, did you get it in England?"

Mrs Brown joined him and looked at the little ornament with a puzzled frown.

"My husband must have got it," she said. "I was away last week and hadn't noticed it before. But I'm always coming back and finding curios and antiques all over the place. My husband's mad on them. He's always bringing them home . . ."

"Most interesting," said Mr Markson, still examining the figure. "*Most* interesting . . . I must have a talk with your husband about it. I quite understood that mine was unique—"

There came the sound of the tea-gong, and Mrs Brown ushered them into the dining-room.

William's extraordinary behaviour was quite forgotten except by the kind old lady, who was so worried by it that she scarcely ate anything at all.

As soon as the guests were safely shut into the dining-room, William slid down the banisters and into the drawing-room. His face wore a look of strained anxiety. He must take the thing away at once before old Markie spotted it. He only hoped that he hadn't spotted it before tea, but he didn't think so because the tea-bell had gone almost at once. But he wondered whether that old lady had told his mother about his eyes and legs. Crumbs, he simply didn't get a bit of peace – just one thing after another.

He slipped the little image into his pocket and, peering carefully around the hall to make sure that the coast was clear, crept stealthily out of the front door and set off at a run down the drive and into the road. He felt a great relief. The danger was over. Old Markie was safely at tea. He could easily slip the thing into its place again before old Markie returned.

"It's William Brown, isn't it? William dear!"

He turned with an inward groan. It was Mrs Franks, a friend of his mother's.

Unchilled by his expression, she greeted him effusively.

"Just the little boy I wanted to meet," she said with an all-embracing smile. "I want you to take a note to your mother, dear. Just come back to me and I'll write it out for you."

William muttered something about being "busy" and "in a hurry," and "come along later," but it was useless. She put an arm affectionately upon his shoulder and gently drew him along with her.

"I know you want to be mother's helpful little man," she coaxed, ignoring his ferocious scowl, "and I won't keep you one minute longer than I must from your toys and little friends."

William gulped eloquently and, his face flaming with fury, allowed himself to be led down the road. The only satisfaction he allowed himself was a vigorous ducking out of the circle of her arm. He accompanied her in silence, refusing even to satisfy her curiosity as to how he did and his mother did and how his father did and how Ethel did and wasn't it a sudden change in the weather.

The hateful image seemed to be shouting its existence aloud to all the world from its inadequate hiding-place in William's pocket. And every minute made the return of it more dangerous. Every minute old Markie might be going back to his lair. He sat, fuming inwardly in Mrs Franks' drawing-room while she wrote the note at her bureau, his hands on his bare knees, his muddy boots planted firmly on the carpet, his tousled head turned in the direction of the window, his freckled face set in a stern frown.

Then, suddenly, his eyes filled with horror and his jaw dropped open. Old Markie was coming down the road again; old Markie was coming in at the drive of Mrs Franks' house; old Markie was ringing the bell. A sudden panic came over William. Not only did the Chinese image protrude conspicuously from his pocket, but its head was distinctly visible. Anything rather than be caught by old Markie with the thing in his pocket. He took it out of his pocket and slipped it with feverish haste upon the top of the piano behind a small Dresden china shepherdess. Then he sat staring in front of him, his face vying with the Chinese image's in blankness and immobility.

Mrs Franks had not noticed his movement, she went on writing.

Mr Markson entered. He threw a quick glance at William and then proceeded to ignore him. Another small boy, perhaps a pupil at his own school – he didn't know and didn't care. The less notice taken of small boys the better. His business with Mrs Franks concerned the coming village pageant which he was organising. But in the middle of their conversation his eyes wandered to the piano and his voice died away. His eyes dilated. His jaw dropped open. William still stared fixedly in front of him. William's expression of blankness verged on imbecility.

"Er – excuse me," said Mr Markson, advancing to the piano, "but – er – most extraordinary. *Most* extraordinary."

He picked up the little image and examined it. His perplexity increased. "*Most* extraordinary – three in the same village and I was *assured* that mine was unique."

WILLIAM STILL STARED FIXEDLY IN FRONT OF HIM AS MR
MARKSON PICKED UP THE LITTLE IMAGE AND EXAMINED IT.

"To what do you refer, Mr Markson?" said Mrs
Franks pleasantly.

"This little Chinese image on the piano," said Mr
Markson. He sounded like a man in a dream.

"Oh, the shepherdess!" said Mrs Franks brightly,
fixing her short-sighted eyes vaguely in the direction of
the piano.

"It's not a shepherdess, pardon me," said Mr Markson
courteously, "it's a Chinese god."

MR MARKSON'S PERPLEXITY INCREASED. "MOST
EXTRAORDINARY!" HE SAID.

"Fancy that now," said Mrs Franks in genuine surprise,
"and I always thought that it was a shepherdess."

"Not at all, not at all," said Mr Markson, still examining the figure. "Forgive the impertinence, Mrs Franks,
but did you get the figure at a curio dealer's?"

"No, Mr Markson, my aunt left it to me, but" – Mrs
Franks was certainly surprised – "fancy it being a Chinese
god, and all these years I've thought it was a shepherdess
and so did my aunt."

The striking of the clock of the village church
reminded Mr Markson that time was getting on and that

he wanted to take a short walk before dinner, so after receiving from Mrs Franks a repeated assurance that she would be *proud* indeed to impersonate an early Saxon matron, provided, of course, that the costume was – er – suitable, Mr Markson departed with one last long perplexed look at the Chinese image on the piano. William, who had been holding his breath for the last few minutes, emitted a long, resonant sigh of relief which fluttered all the papers on Mrs Franks' bureau.

"William darling, don't *blow* like that," said Mrs Franks reprovingly. "I'll just address the envelope, dear, and then you can take it."

She sat down again at her bureau, with her back to him, and William, seizing his opportunity, slipped the Chinese image again into his pocket.

"Here it is, dear," said Mrs Franks, handing it to him.

Then she went over to the piano, took up the Dresden china shepherdess and examined it from every angle.

"A Chinese god," she said at last. "What an extraordinary idea! No, I don't agree with him at all. Not at all, dear, do you? A Chinese god" – her amazement increased – "why, nothing about it even remotely suggests the Orient to me. Does it to you, dear? The man must suffer from some defect in his sight."

William murmured something inaudible, took a hasty farewell of her, seized the note, and hurried out into the road.

Old Markie had said that he was going for a walk before dinner. That would give him plenty of time to put the thing back. Crumbs! He'd had an awful few minutes in Mrs Franks' drawing-room, but it was all over now. He'd just put the thing back where he'd got it, and – and

– well, he'd never go into old Markie's house again for
anything. He was pretty sure of *that*. Crumbs! He
wouldn't, indeed.

He stopped at the gate of The Nest and looked up
and down the road. The road was empty. With a quickly
beating heart he went up the drive. The French windows
were shut, but the front door was open. He slipped into
the hall. He took the Chinese image out of his pocket,
and stood for one moment irresolute holding it in his
hand. Then, the door of the room at the back of the hall
opened and Mr Markson came out into the hall.

Mr Markson had thought that the clouds were gathering and had decided not to go for a walk before dinner
after all.

"Who's that?" he bellowed. "What do you want, boy?
Come in! Come in!"

William slowly advanced to the back room still
holding the Chinese figure in his hand.

Mr Markson looked him up and down. William silently implored the earth to open and swallow him up, but
the earth callously refused.

A light of recognition dawned in Mr Markson's eyes.

"Why, you're Mrs Brown's boy," he said.

"Yes, sir," said William tonelessly.

Then Mr Markson's eye fell upon the Chinese figure
which William was vainly trying to conceal with his hands.

"What!" he began, "you've brought her Chinese
figure?"

William moistened his lips.

"Yes, sir. She – she's – she's sent it, sir."

"*Sent* it?" said Mr Markson. His eyes gleamed with
the greed of the collector. "You mean – *sent* it?"

"Yes, sir," said William with sudden inspiration. "She's sent it to you – to keep, sir."

"But how *extraordinarily* kind," burst out Mr Markson. "I must write to her at once. How very kind! I must – wait a minute. There's still the third. I'll write to Mrs Franks, too. I'll ask Mrs Franks if she can possibly trace the origin of her piece." He was speaking to himself rather than to William. "I'll just hint that I'd be willing to buy it should she ever wish to sell. Sit down there and wait, boy."

William sat down and waited in silence while Mr Markson wrote at his desk. William stared desperately in front of him. Crumbs! Things were getting in more of a mess every minute. He didn't see how he could possibly get out of it now. He was in it – right up to the neck. But – Mr Markson fastened up the envelope, addressed it, and turned to William.

Just then a maid entered with the evening post on a tray. Mr Markson took it. She retired and Mr Markson read his letters.

"Bother!" he said, "here's a letter that *must* be answered by tonight's post. Do something for me, boy. Take this figure and put it on the table in the front room with its fellow and then take this note to Mrs Franks, will you?"

"Yes, sir," said William meekly.

Mr Markson sat down at his bureau. William went quickly and gratefully from the room. In the hall he stopped to consider the situation. Mr Markson would expect an answer from Mrs Franks. He might even ring her up about it. There would be awkward complications, awkward for William that is— And suddenly yet another inspiration came to him. He pocketed the image again and set off down the road. He walked for a few yards, turned back, walked up again to the front door of The Nest and into the back room. Mr Markson was still writing his letter. William took the Chinese figure out of his pocket.

"Mrs Franks sent you this, sir," he said in his most expressionless voice, staring in front of him fixedly.

Mr Markson's face beamed with joy.

"*Sent* it?" he gasped.

"Yes, sir," said William, speaking monotonously, as though he were repeating a lesson. "An' she said please will you not write to her about it or thank her or ever mention it to her please, sir."

At the conclusion of this breathless speech William paled and blinked, still staring fixedly before him. But old Markie beamed with joy.

"What delicacy of feeling that displays," he said. "A lesson indeed to the cruder manners of this age. How – how *exceptionally* kind!" He held the china piece on his hand. "The third! What almost incredible good fortune! The third! Now to put it with its two fellows."

He walked across to the front room and entered it. He looked from the image in his hand to the empty table where that image had stood only a few hours ago. He looked from table to image, from image to table, and again from table to image. Then he turned for an explanation from William.

But William was no longer there.

CHAPTER FOUR

WILLIAM LEADS A BETTER LIFE

IF YOU GO far enough back it was Mr Strong, William's form master, who was responsible for the whole thing. Mr Strong set, for homework, more French than it was convenient for William to learn. It happened that someone had presented William with an electric motor, and the things one can do with an electric motor are endless.

Who would waste the precious hours of a summer evening over French verbs with an electric motor simply crying out to be experimented on? Certainly not William.

It wasn't as if there was any *sense* in French verbs. They had been deliberately invented by someone with a grudge against the race of boys – someone probably who'd slipped on a concealed slide or got in the way of a snow-ball or foolishly come within the danger zone of a catapult. Anyway, whoever it was had devised a mean form of revenge by inventing French verbs and, somehow or other, persuading schoolmasters to adopt them as one of their choicest tortures.

"Well, I never *will* wanter use 'em," said William to his mother when she brought forward the time-honoured argument. "I don't wanter talk to *any* French folks, an' if

they wanter talk to me they can learn English. English's
's easy 's easy to talk. It's *silly* havin' other langwidges. I
don' see why all the other countries shun't learn English
'stead of us learnin' other langwidges with no *sense* in
'em. English's *sense*."

This speech convinced him yet more firmly of the
foolishness of wasting his precious hours of leisure on
such futile study, so he devoted all his time and energy
to the electric motor. There was some *sense* in the electric
motor. William spent a very happy evening.

In the morning, however, things somehow seemed
different. He lay in bed and considered the matter. There
was no doubt that Mr Strong could make himself
extremely disagreeable over French verbs.

William remembered that he had threatened to make
himself more disagreeable than usual if William did not
know them "next time". This was "next time" and
William did not know them. William had not even
attempted to learn them. The threats of Mr Strong had
seemed feeble, purposeless, contemptible things last night
when the electric motor threw its glamour over the whole
world. This morning they didn't. They seemed suddenly
much more real than the electric motor.

But surely it was possible to circumvent them. William
was not the boy to give in weakly to any fate. He heard
his mother's door opening, and, assuming an expression
of intense suffering, called weakly, "Mother." Mrs Brown
entered the room fully dressed.

"Aren't you up yet, William?" she said: "Be quick or
you'll be late for school."

William intensified yet further his expression of suffering.

"I don' think I feel quite well enough to go to school this morning, mother, dear," he said faintly.

Mrs Brown looked distressed. He had employed the ruse countless times before, but it never failed of its effect upon Mrs Brown. The only drawback was that Mr Brown, who was still about the house, was of a less trustful and compassionate nature.

Mrs Brown smoothed his pillow. "Poor little boy," she said tenderly, "where is the pain?"

"All over," said William, playing for safety.

"Dear! dear!" said Mrs Brown, much perturbed, as she left the room. "I'll just go and fetch the thermometer."

William disliked the thermometer. It was a soulless, unsympathetic thing. Sometimes, of course, a hot-water bottle, judiciously placed, would enlist its help, but that was not always easy to arrange.

To William's dismay his father entered the room with the thermometer.

"Well, William," he said cheerfully, "I hear you're too ill to go to school. That's a great pity, isn't it. I'm sure it's a great grief to you?"

William turned up his eyes. "Yes, father," he said dutifully and suspiciously.

"Now where exactly is the pain and what sort of pain is it?"

William knew from experience that descriptions of non-existent pains are full of pitfalls. By a master-stroke he avoided them.

"It hurts me to talk," he said.

"What sort of pain does it hurt you with?" said his father brutally.

William made some inarticulate noises, then closed his eyes with a moan of agony.

"I'll just step round and fetch the doctor," said Mr Brown, still quite cheerful.

The doctor lived next door. William considered this a great mistake. He disliked the close proximity of doctors. They were equally annoying in real and imaginary diseases.

William made little brave reassuring noises to inform his father that he'd rather the doctor wasn't troubled and it was all right, and please no one was to bother about him, and he'd just stay in bed and probably be all right by the afternoon. But his father had already gone.

William lay in bed and considered his position.

Well, he was going to stick to it, anyway. He'd just make noises to the doctor, and they couldn't say he hadn't got a pain where he said he had if they didn't know where he said he had one. His mother came in and took his temperature. Fate was against him. There was no hot-water bottle handy. But he squeezed it as hard as he could in a vague hope that that would have some effect on it.

"It's normal, dear," said his mother, relieved. "I'm so glad."

He made a sinister noise to imply that the malady was too deep-seated to be shown by an ordinary thermometer.

He could hear the doctor and his father coming up the stairs. They were laughing and talking. William, forgetting the imaginary nature of his complaint, felt a wave of indignation and self-pity.

The doctor came in breezily. "Well, young man," he said, "what's the trouble?"

William made his noise. By much practice he was

becoming an expert at the noise. It implied an intense desire to explain his symptoms, thwarted by physical incapability, and it thrilled with suffering bravely endured.

"Can't speak – is that it?" said the doctor.

"Yes, that's it," said William, forgetting his rôle for the minute.

"Well – open your mouth, and let's have a look at your throat," said the doctor.

William opened his mouth and revealed his throat. The doctor inspected the recesses of that healthy and powerful organ.

"I see," he said at last. "Yes – very bad. But I can operate here and now, fortunately. I'm afraid I can't give an anaesthetic in this case, and I'm afraid it will be rather painful – but I'm sure he's a brave boy."

William went pale and looked around desperately. French verbs were preferable to this.

"I'll wait just three minutes," said the doctor kindly. "Occasionally in cases like this the patient recovers his voice quite suddenly." He took out his watch. William's father was watching the scene with an air of enjoyment that William found maddening. "I'll give him just three minutes," went on the doctor, "and if the patient hasn't recovered the power of speech by then, I'll operate—"

The patient decided hastily to recover the power of speech.

"I can speak now," he said with an air of surprise. "Isn't it funny? I can talk quite ordinary now. It came on quite sudden."

"No pain anywhere?" said the doctor.

"No," said the patient quickly.

The patient's father stepped forward.

"Then you'd better get up as quickly as you can," he said. "You'll be late for school, but doubtless they'll know how to deal with that."

They did know how to deal with that. They knew, too, how to deal with William's complete ignorance on the subject of French verbs. Excuses (and William had many – some of them richly ingenious) were of no avail. He went home to lunch embittered and disillusioned with life.

"You'd think knowin' how to work a motor engine'd be more *useful* than sayin' French verbs," he said. "S'pose I turned out an engineer – well, wot use'd French verbs be to me 'n I'd *have* to know how to work a motor engine. An' I was so ill this mornin' that the doctor wanted to do an operate on me, but I said I *can't* miss school an' get all behind the others, an' I came, awful ill, an' all they did was to carry on something terrible 'cause I was jus' a minute or two late an' jus' ha'n't had time to do those old French verbs that aren't no *use* to anyone—"

Ginger, Henry and Douglas sympathised with him for some time, then began to discuss the history lesson. The history master, feeling for the moment as bored with Edward the Sixth as were most of his class, had given them a graphic account of the life of St Francis of Assisi. He had spent the Easter holidays at Assisi. William, who had been engaged in executing creditable caricatures of Mr Strong and the doctor, had paid little attention, but Ginger remembered it all. It had been such a welcome change from William the Conqueror. William began to follow the discussion.

"Yes, but why'd he do it?" he said.

"Well, he jus' got kind of fed up with things an' he

had visions an' things an' he took some things of his father's to sell to get money to start it—"

"*Crumbs!*" interpolated William. "Wasn't his father mad?"

"Yes, but that din't matter. He was a saint, was Saint Francis, so he could sell his father's things if he liked, an' he 'n his frien's took the money an' got funny long sort of clothes an' went an' lived away in a little house by themselves, an' he uster preach to animals an' to people an' call everythin' 'brother' an' 'sister', and they cooked all their own stuff to eat an'—"

"Jolly fine it sounds," said William enviously, "an' did their people let 'em?"

"They couldn't stop 'em," said Ginger. "An' Francis, he was the head one, an' the others all called themselves Franciscans, an' they built churches an' things."

They had reached the gate of William's house now and William turned in slowly.

"G'bye till this afternoon," called the others cheerfully.

Lunch increased still further William's grievances. No one inquired after his health, though he tried to look pale and ill, and refused a second helping of rice pudding with a meaning, "No, thank you, not today. I would if I felt all right, thank you very much." Even that elicited no anxious inquiries. No one, thought William, as he finished up the rice pudding in secret in the larder afterwards, no one else in the world, surely, had such a callous family. It would just serve them right to lose him altogether. It would just serve them right if he went off like St Francis and never came back.

He met Henry and Ginger and Douglas again as usual on the way to school.

"Beastly ole 'rithmetic," said Henry despondently.

"Yes, an' then beastly ole jography," sighed Douglas.

"Well," said William, "let's not go. I've been thinkin' a lot about that Saint man. I'd a lot sooner be a saint an' build things an' cook things an' preach to things than keep goin' to school an' learnin' the same ole things day after day an' day after day – all things like French verbs without any *sense* in them. I'd much sooner be a saint, wun't you?"

The other Outlaws looked doubtful, yet as though attracted by the idea.

"They wun't let us," said Henry.

"They can't stop us bein' saints," said William piously, "an' doin' good an' preachin' – not if we have visions, an' I feel's if I could have visions quite easy."

The Outlaws had slackened their pace.

"What'd we have to do first?" said Ginger.

"Sell some of our fathers' things to get money," said William firmly. "'S all right," he went on, anticipating possible objections, "he did, so I s'pose anyone can if they're settin' out to be saints – of course it would be different if we was jus' stealin', but bein' saints makes it diff'rent. Stands to reason saints can't steal."

"Well, what'd we do *then*?" said Douglas.

"Then we find a place an' get the right sort of clothes to wear—"

"Seems sort of a waste of money," said Henry sternly, "spendin' it on *clothes*. What sort of clothes were they?"

"He showed us a picture," said Ginger, "don' you

remember? Sort of long things goin' right down to his feet."

"Dressing-gowns'd do," said Douglas excitedly.

"No, you're thinkin' of detectives," said Henry firmly; "detectives wear dressing-gowns."

"No," said William judicially. "I don' see why dressing-gowns shun't do. Then we can save the money an' spend it on things to eat."

"Where'll we live?"

"We oughter build a place, but till we've built it we can live in the old barn."

"Where'll we get the animals to preach to?"

"Well, there's a farm just across the way from the barn, you know. We can start on Jumble an' then go on to the farm ones when we've had some practice."

"An' what'll we be called? We can't be the Outlaws now we're saints, I s'pose?"

"What were they called?"

"Franciscans . . . After Francis – he was the head one."

"Well, if there's goin' to be any head one," said William in a tone that precluded any argument on the subject, "if there's going to be any head one, I'm going to be him."

None of them denied to William the position of leader. It was his by right. He had always led, and he was a leader they were proud to follow.

"Well, they just put 'cans' on to the end of his name," said Henry. "Franciscans. So we'll be Williamcans—"

"Sounds kind of funny," said Ginger dubiously.

"I think it sounds jolly fine," said William proudly. "I vote we start tomorrow, 'cause it's rather late to start today, an' anyway, it's Saturday tomorrow, so we can get

well started for Monday, 'cause they're sure to make a
fuss about our not turnin' up at school on Monday. You
all come to the old barn d'rectly after breakfast tomorrow an' bring your dressing-gowns an' somethin' of
your father's to sell—"

The first meeting of the Williamcans was held directly
after breakfast the next morning. They had all left notes
dictated by William on their bedroom mantelpieces
announcing that they were now saints and had left home
for ever.

They deposited their dressing-gowns on the floor of
the old barn and then inspected the possessions that they
had looted from their unsuspecting fathers. William had
appropriated a pair of slippers, not because he thought
their absence would be undetected (far from it) or
because he thought they would realise vast wealth (again
far from it), but it happened that they were kept in the
fender-box of the morning-room, and William had found
himself alone there for a few minutes that morning, and
slippers can be concealed quite easily beneath one's coat.
He could have more easily appropriated something of his
mother's, but William liked to do things properly. Saint
Francis had sold something of his father's, so Saint
William would do the same. Douglas took from his pocket
an inkstand, purloined from his father's desk; Ginger had
two ties and Henry a pair of gloves.

They looked at their spoils with proud satisfaction.

"We oughter get a good deal of money for *these*," said
William. "How much did *he* get, d'you know?"

"No, he never said," said Ginger.

"We'd better not put on our saint robes yet – not till

we've been down to the village to sell the things. Then we'll put 'em on an' start preachin' an' things."

"Din' we oughter wear round-hoop-sort-of-things on our heads?" said Henry. "They do in pictures. What d'you call 'em? – Halos."

"You don' get *them* till you're dead," said Ginger with an air of wisdom.

"Well, I don't see what good they are to anyone *dead*," said Henry, rather aggrieved.

"No, we've gotter do things *right*," said William sternly. "If the real saints waited till they was dead, we will, too. Anyway, let's go an' sell the things first. An' remember call everything else 'brother' or 'sister'."

"*Everything?*"

"Yes – *he* did – the other man did."

"You've gotter call me *Saint* William now, Ginger."

"All right, you call me Saint Ginger."

"All right, I'm goin' to – Saint Ginger—"

"Saint William."

"All right."

"Well, where you goin' to sell the slippers?"

"*Brother* slippers," corrected William. "Well, I'm goin' to sell brother slippers at Mr Marsh's 'f he'll buy 'em."

"An I'll take brother ties along, too," said Ginger. "An' Henry take brother gloves, an' Douglas brother inkstand."

"*Sister* inkstand," said Douglas. "William—"

"Saint William," corrected William, patiently.

"Well, Saint William said we could call things brother *or* sister, an' my inkstand's goin' to be sister."

"*Swank!*" said St Ginger severely, "always wanting to be diff'rent from other people!"

78

Mr Marsh kept a second-hand shop at the end of the village. In his window reposed side by side a motley collection of battered and despised household goods.

He had a less optimistic opinion of the value of brothers slippers and ties and gloves and sister inkstand than the saints.

He refused to allow them more than sixpence each.

"*Mean!*" exploded St William indignantly as soon as they had emerged from Mr Marsh's dingy little sanctum to the village street and the light of day. "I call him sim'ly *mean*. That's what *I* call him."

"I s'pose now we're saints," said St Ginger piously, "that we've gotter forgive folks what wrong us like that."

"I'm not goin' to be *that* sort of a saint," said St William firmly.

Back at the barn they donned their dressing-gowns, St Henry still grumbling at not being able to wear the "little hoop" on his head.

"Now what d'we do *first?*" said St Ginger energetically, as he fastened the belt of his dressing-gown.

"Well, anyway, why can't we cut little bits of our hair at the top like they have in pictures?" said St Henry disconsolately, "that'd be better than *nothin'*."

This idea rather appealed to the saints. St Douglas discovered a penknife and began to operate at once on St Henry, but the latter saint's yells of agony soon brought the proceedings to a premature end.

"Well, *you* s'gested it," said St Douglas, rather hurt, "an' I was doin' it as gently as I could."

"*Gently!*" groaned Henry, still nursing his saintly head. "You were tearing it out by the roots."

"Well, come *on!*" said St Ginger impatiently, "let's begin now. What did you say we were goin' to do first?"

"Preachin' to animals is the first thing," said William in his most business-like manner. "I've got Brother Jumble here. Ginger – I mean St Ginger, you hold Brother Jumble while I preach to him 'cause he's not used to it, an' he might try to run away, an' St Henry an' St Douglas go out an' preach to birds. The St Francis man did a lot of preachin' to birds. They came an' sat on his arms. See if you can gettem to do that. Well now, let's start. Ginger – I mean St Ginger – you catch hold of Brother Jumble."

Henry and Douglas departed. Douglas's dressing-gown, made by a thrifty mother with a view to Douglas's further growth, was slightly too big and tripped him over every few steps. Henry's was made of bath towelling and was rather conspicuous in design. They made their way slowly across a field and into a neighbouring wood.

St Ginger encircled the reluctant Jumble with his arms, and St William stood up to preach.

"Dearly beloved Jumble—" he began.

"Brother Jumble," corrected St Ginger, with triumph. He liked to catch the founder of the order tripping.

Jumble, under the delusion that something was expected of him, sat up and begged.

"Dearly beloved Brother Jumble," repeated William. He stopped and cleared his throat in the manner of all speakers who are not sure what to say next.

Jumble, impatient of the other saint's encircling arms, tried another trick, that of standing on his head. Standing on his head was the title given to the performance by Jumble's owner. In reality it consisted of rubbing the top

ST WILLIAM STOOD UP TO PREACH TO THE RELUCTANT JUMBLE.
"DEARLY BELOVED JUMBLE," HE BEGAN.

of his head on the ground. None of his legs left the
ground, but William always called it "Jumble standing on
his head", and was inordinately proud of it.

"Look at him," he said, "isn't that jolly clever? An'
no one told him to. Jus' did it without anyone tellin' him

to. I bet there's not many dogs like him. I bet he's the cleverest dog there is in England. I wun't mind sayin' he's the cleverest dog there is in the world. I wun't—"

"I thought you was preachin' to him, not talkin' about him," said St Ginger, sternly. Ginger, who was not allowed to possess a dog, tired occasionally of hearing William sing the praises of his.

"Oh, yes," said St William with less enthusiasm. "I'll start all over again. Dearly beloved Brother Jumble – I say, what did that St Francis *say* to the animals?"

"Dunno," said St Ginger vaguely, "I s'pect he jus' told 'em to – well, to do good an' that sort of thing."

"Dearly beloved Brother Jumble," said William again, "you mus' – do good an – an' stop chasin' cats. Why," he said proudly, "there's not a cat in this village that doesn't run when it sees Jumble comin'. I bet he's the best dog for chasin' cats anywhere round *this* part of England. I bet—"

Jumble, seizing his moment for escape, tore himself from St Ginger's unwary arms, and leapt up ecstatically at William.

"Good old Jumble," said the saint affectionately. "Good old boy!"

At this point the other two saints returned.

"Well, did you find any birds?" said St William.

"There was heaps of birds," said St Douglas in an exasperated tone of voice, "but the minute I started preachin' they all flew off. They din' seem to know how to *act* with saints. They din' seem to know they'd got to sit on our arms an' things. Made us feel *mad* – anyway, we gotter thrush's egg and Henry – I mean St Henry – jus' wanted one of those—"

"Well," said St William rather sternly, "I don' think it's the right thing for saints to do – to go preachin' to birds an' then takin' their eggs – I mean their brother eggs."

"There was *lots* more," said Henry. "They *like* you jus' takin' one. It makes it less trouble for 'em hatchin' 'em out."

"Well, anyway," said William, "let's get on with this animal business. P'raps the tame ones'll be better. Let's go across to Jenks' farm an' try on them."

They crept rather cautiously into the farmyard. The feud between Farmer Jenks and the Outlaws was one of long standing. He would probably not realise that the Williamcans were a saintly organisation whose every action was inspired by a love of mankind. He would probably imagine that they were still the old unregenerate Outlaws.

"I'll do brother cows," said St William, "an' St Ginger do brother pigs, and St Douglas do brother goats, an' St Henry do sister hens."

They approached their various audiences. Ginger leant over the pigsty. Then he turned to William, who was already striking an attitude before his congregation of cows, and said: "I say, what've I gotter *say* to 'em?"

At that moment brother goat, being approached too nearly by St Douglas, butted the saintly stomach, and St Douglas sat down suddenly and heavily. Brother goat, evidently enjoying this form of entertainment, returned to the charge. St Douglas fled to the accompaniment of an uproarious farmyard commotion.

Farmer Jenks appeared, and, seeing his old enemies, the Outlaws, actually within his precincts, he uttered a yell of fury and darted down upon them. The saints fled

WILLIAM WAS ALREADY STRIKING AN ATTITUDE BEFORE HIS
CONGREGATION OF COWS.

swiftly, St Douglas holding up his too flowing robe as he
went. Brother goat had given St Douglas a good start and
he reached the farm first.

"Well," said St William, panting, "I've *finished* with
preachin' to animals. They must have changed a good bit
since *his* time. That's all *I* can say."

"Well, what'll we do *now?*" said St Ginger.

"I should almost think it's time for dinner," said
William. "Must be after two, I should think."

No one knew the time. Henry possessed a watch which had been given to him by a great-uncle. Though it may possibly have had some value as an antique, it had not gone for over twenty years. Henry, however, always wore it, and generally remembered to move its hands to a correct position whenever he passed a clock. This took a great deal of time and trouble, but Henry was proud of his watch and liked it to be as nearly right as possible. He consulted it now. He had put it right by his family's hall clock as he came out after breakfast, so its fingers stood at half-past nine. He returned it to his pocket hastily before the others could see the position of the fingers.

"Yes," he said, with the air of an oracle, "it's about

FARMER JENKS UTTERED A YELL OF FURY AND BORE DOWN
UPON THE OUTLAWS. DOUGLAS FLED SWIFTLY.

dinner-time." Though they all knew that Henry's watch had never gone, yet it had a certain prestige.

"Well, we've gotter *buy* our dinner," said William. "'S'pose two of us goes down to the village, an' buys it now with the two shillings we got for sellin' our fathers' things. We've gotter buy all our meals now like what *they* did."

"Well, how d'we get the money when we've finished this? We can't go *on* sellin' our fathers' things. They'd get so mad."

"We beg from folks after that," said Ginger, who was the only one who had paid much attention to the story of the life of St Francis.

"Well, I bet they won't give us much if *I* know 'em," said William bitterly. "I bet both folks *an'* animals must've been nicer in those times."

It was decided that Douglas and Henry should go down to the village to purchase provisions for the meal. It was decided also that they should go in their dressing-gowns.

"*They* always did," said Ginger firmly, "and folks may's well get used to us goin' about like that."

"Oh, yes!" said Douglas bitterly. "'S easy to talk like that when you're not goin' down to the shop."

Mr Moss, the proprietor of the village sweet-shop, held his sides with laughter when he saw them.

"Well, I never!" he said. "Well, I never! What boys you are for a joke, to be sure!"

"It's not a joke," said Henry. "We're Williamcans."

Douglas had caught sight of the clock on the desk behind the counter.

"I say!" he said. "It's only eleven o'clock."

Henry took out his watch.

"Oh, yes," he said, as if he had made a mistake when he looked at it before.

For their midday meal the two saints purchased a large bag of chocolate creams, another of bull's-eyes, and, to form the more solid part of the meal, four cream buns.

Ginger and William and Jumble were sitting comfortably in the old barn when the two emissaries returned.

"*We've* had a nice time!" exploded St Henry. "All the boys in the place runnin' after us an' shoutin' at us."

"You should've just stood still an' *preached* to 'em," said the founder of the order calmly.

"*Preached* to 'em!" repeated Henry. "They wun't have listened. They was shoutin' an' throwin' things an' running at us."

"What'd you do?"

"Run," said the gallant saint simply. "An' Douglas has tore his robe, an' I've fallen in the mud in mine."

"Well, they've gotter last you all the rest of your life," said St William, "so you oughter take more care of 'em," and added with more interest, "what've you got for dinner?"

They displayed their purchases and their choice was warmly and unanimously approved by the saints.

"Wish we'd thought of something to drink," said Henry.

But William, with a smile of pride, brought out from his pocket a bottle of dark liquid.

"I *thought* of that," he said, holding it out with a flourish, "have a drink of brother lik'rice water."

Not to be outdone, Douglas took up one of the bags.

"An' have a sister cream bun," he said loudly.

When they had eaten and drunk to repletion they rested for a short time from their labours. William had meant to fill in time by preaching to Jumble, but decided instead to put Jumble through his tricks.

"I s'pose they *know* now at home that we've gone for good," said Henry with a sigh.

Ginger looked out of the little window anxiously.

"Yes. I only hope to goodness they won't come an' try to fetch us back," he said.

But he need not have troubled. Each family thought that the missing member was having lunch with one of the others, and felt no anxiety, only a great relief. And none of the notes upon the mantelpieces had been found.

"What'll we do *now?*" said William, rousing himself at last.

"*They* built a church," said Ginger.

"Crumbs!" said William, taken aback. "Well, we can't do that, can we?"

"Oh, I dunno," said Ginger vaguely, "jus' keep on putting stones on each other. It was quite a little church."

"Well, it'd take us more'n quite a little time."

"Yes, but we've gotter do *something* 'stead of goin' to school, an' we may's well do that."

"'S almost as bad as goin' to school," said William gloomily. "An' where'd they get the stones?"

"They jus' found 'em lying about."

"Well, come on," said William, rising with a resigned air and gathering the folds of his dressing-gown about him, "let's see 'f we can find any lyin' about."

They wandered down the road. They still wore their dressing-gowns, but they wore them with a sheepish air and went cautiously and furtively. Already their affection for their saintly garb was waning. Fortunately, the road was deserted. They looked up and down, then St Ginger gave a yell of triumph and pointed up the road. The road was being mended, and there lay by the roadside, among other materials, a little heap of wooden bricks. Moreover, the bricks were unguarded and unattended.

It was the British workman's dinner hour, and the British workman was spending it in the nearest pub.

"Crumbs!" said the Williamcans in delight.

They fell upon the wooden bricks and bore them off in triumph. Soon they had a pile of them just outside the barn where they had resolved to build the church – almost enough, the head of the order decided, to begin on. But as they paid their last visit for bricks they met a little crowd of other children, who burst into loud jeering cries.

"Look at 'em ... Dear little girlies ... wearin' nice long pinnies ... Oh, my! Oh, *don'* they look sweet? Hello, little darlin's!"

William flung aside his saintly robe and closed with the leader. The other saints closed with the others. Quite an interesting fight ensued. The saints, smaller in number and size than the other side, most decidedly got the best of it, though not without many casualties. The other side took to its heels.

St William, without much enthusiasm, picked his saintly robe up from the mud and began to put it on.

"Don' see much *sense* in wearin' these things," he said.

"You ought to have *preached* to 'em, not fought 'em," said Ginger severely.

"Well, I bet *he* wun't've preached to 'em if they'd started makin' fun of him. He'd've fought 'em all right."

"No, he wun't," said Ginger firmly, "he din't b'lieve in fightin'."

William's respect for his prototype, already on the wane, waned still farther. But he did not lightly relinquish anything he had once undertaken.

"Well, anyway," he said, "let's get a move on buildin' that church."

They returned to the field and their little pile of bricks.

But the British workman had also returned from his dinner hour at the nearest pub, and had discovered the disappearance of the larger part of his material. With lurid oaths he had tracked them down and came upon the saints just as they had laboriously laid the first row of bricks for the first wall. He burst upon them with fury.

They did not stay to argue. They fled. Henry cast aside his splendid robe of multi-coloured bath towelling into a ditch to accelerate his flight. The British workman tired first. He went back after throwing a brick at their retreating forms and informing them lustily that he knew their fathers an' he'd go an' tell them, danged if he wouldn't, and they'd find themselves in jail – saucy little 'ounds – danged if they wouldn't.

The Williamcans waited till all was clear before they emerged from their hiding-places and gathered together dejectedly in the barn. William and Ginger had sustained black eyes and bleeding noses as the result of the fight with the village children. Douglas had fallen during the flight from the British workman and caught Henry on his ankle, and he limped painfully. Their faces had acquired an extraordinary amount of dirt.

They sat down and surveyed each other.

"Seems to me," said William, "it's a *wearin'* kind of life."

It was cold. It had begun to rain.

"Brother rain," remarked Ginger brightly.

"Yes, an' I should think it's about sister tea-time," said William dejectedly; "an' what we goin' to buy it – her – with? How're we goin' to get money?"

"I've got sixpence at home," said Henry. "I mean I've gotter brother sixpence at home."

But William had lost his usual optimism.

"Well, that won't keep all of us for the rest of our lives, will it?" he said; "an' I don't feel like startin' beggin' after the time I've had today. I haven't got much *trust* in folks."

"Henry – I mean, St Henry – oughter give his brother sixpence to the poor," said Ginger piously. "*They* uster give all their money to the poor."

"*Give* it?" said William incredulously. "An' get nothin' back for it?"

"No – jus' give it," said Ginger.

William thought deeply for a minute.

"Well," he said at last, voicing the opinion of the whole order, "I'm jus' about sick of bein' a saint. I'd sooner be a pirate or a Red Indian any day."

The rest looked relieved.

"Yes, I've had *enough*," said William, "and let's stop callin' each other saints an' brothers an' sisters an' wearin' dressing-gowns. There's no *sense* in it. An' I'm almost dyin' of cold an' hunger an' I'm goin' home."

They set off homeward through the rain, cold and wet and bruised and very hungry. The saintly repast of cream buns and chocolate creams and bull's-eyes, though enjoyable at the time, had proved singularly unsustaining.

But their troubles were not over.

As they went through the village they stopped in front of Mr Marsh's shop window. There in the very middle were William's father's slippers, Douglas' father's inkstand, Ginger's father's tie and Henry's father's gloves – all marked at 1/-. The hearts of the Williamcans stood still. Their fathers would probably not yet have returned from Town. The thought of their seeing their prized possessions reposing in Mr Marsh's window marked 1/- was a horrid one. It had not seemed to matter this morning. This morning they were leaving their homes for ever. It did seem to matter this evening. This evening they were returning to their homes.

They entered the shop and demanded them. Mr Marsh was adamant. In the end Henry fetched his sixpence, William a treasured penknife, Ginger a compass, and Douglas a broken steam engine, and their paternal possessions were handed back.

They went home dejectedly through the rain. The British workman might or might not fulfil his threat of calling on their parents. The saintly career which had looked so roseate in the distance had turned out, as William aptly described it, "wearin'." Life was full of disillusions.

William discovered with relief that his father had not yet come home. He returned the slippers, somewhat damp, to the fender box. He put his muddy dressing-gown beneath the bed. He found his note unopened and unread, still upon the mantelpiece. He tore it up. He tidied himself superficially. He went downstairs.

"Had a nice day, dear?" said his mother.

He disdained to answer the question.

"There's just an hour before tea," she went on; "hadn't you better be doing your homework, dear?"

He considered. One might as well drink of tragedy the very dregs while one was about it. It would be a rotten ending to a rotten day. Besides, there was no doubt about it – Mr Strong was going to make himself very disagreeable indeed, if he didn't know those French verbs for Monday. He might as well . . . If he'd had any idea how rotten it was being a saint he jolly well wouldn't have wasted a whole Saturday over it. He took down a French grammar and sat down moodily before it without troubling to put it right way up.

CHAPTER FIVE

WILLIAM'S
LUCKY DAY

W ILLIAM AND THE other Outlaws sat in the old barn
discussing the latest tragedy that had befallen them.
Tragedies, of course, fell thick and fast upon the Outlaws'
path through life. They waged ceaseless warfare upon the
grown-up world around them and, as was natural, they
frequently came off second best. But this was a special
tragedy. Not only was it a grown-up victory, but it was a
victory that bade fair to make the Outlaws' daily lives
a perpetual martyrdom at the hands of their contemporaries.

Usually, the compensating element of a grown-up
victory was the fact that it concentrated upon them the
sympathy of their associates – a sympathy that not
infrequently found tangible form in the shape of bull's-
eyes or conkers. But this grown-up victory was a victory
that promised to make the lives of the early Christian
martyrs beds of roses in comparison with those of the
Outlaws.

The way it happened was this.

The headmaster of William's school had a cousin who
was a Great Man, and once a year the cousin who was a
Great Man came down to the school to address the boys

of William's school. He possessed, presumably, gifts of a high and noble order, otherwise he would not have been a Great Man, but whatever those gifts may have been they did not include that of holding the interest of small boys. Only the front two rows could ever hear anything he said and not even the front two rows (carefully chosen by the headmaster for their – misleadingly – intelligent expressions) could understand it.

It might be gathered from this that the annual visit of the Great Man was looked forward to without enthusiasm, but this was not the case, for always at the end of the lecture he turned to the headmaster and asked that the boys might be given a half-holiday the next day, and the headmaster, after simulating first of all intense surprise and then doubt and hesitation, while the rows of small boys watched him in breathless suspense, their eyes nearly dropping out of their heads, finally said that they might. Then someone called for three cheers for the Great Man, and the roof quivered. The Great Man was always much gratified by his reception. He always said afterwards that it was delightful to see young boys taking a deep and intelligent interest in such subjects as Astronomy and Egyptology and Geology, and that the cheers with which they greeted the close of the lecture left him with no doubt at all of their appreciation of it. The school in general went very carefully the day before the lecture because it was known that the headmaster disliked granting the half-holiday and with the meanness of his kind would welcome with hidden joy and triumph any excuse for cancelling it. The Great Man's visit was a nervous strain on the headmaster, and his temper was never at its best just then. To begin with, it was an exhausting and nerve-racking task to discover sufficient boys with intelligent expressions to fill the front rows. Then the other boys had to be graded in diminishing degrees of cleanliness and presentability to the back of the hall which the Great Man, being very short-sighted, could not see, and where the least presentable specimens were massed. The Outlaws were always relegated to the very back row. They found no insult in this, but were, on the contrary, grateful for it. By a slight adjustment of their positions they could hide themselves comfortably from the view of Authority, and give their whole attention to such pursuits as conker battles, the swopping of cigarette-cards, or the "racing" of insects conveyed thither in match-boxes for the purpose. But this year a terrible thing had happened.

The Great Man arrived at the village as usual. As usual he stayed with the headmaster. As usual the Outlaws hid behind the hedge to watch him with interest and curiosity as he passed to and from the headmaster's house, going to the village or returning from it. It was unfortunate that the Great Man happened to be wearing a bowler hat that was undoubtedly too small for him. He may have bought it in a hurry and not realised till he had worn it once or twice how much too small it was, and then with dogged British courage and determination decided to wear it out. He may have been honestly labouring under the delusion that it suited and fitted him. The fact remains that when he emerged from the headmaster's gate into the lane the waiting and watching Outlaws drew deep breaths and ejaculated simultaneously;

"Crumbs! Look at his hat!"

"Don't look like a hat at all," commented Douglas.

"Looks like as if he was carryin' an apple on his head," said Ginger.

"William Tell," said Henry with the modest air of one who, without undue ostentation, has no wish to hide his culture and general information under a bushel. "You know, William Tell. What his father shot an apple off his head without touchin' him."

"An' I bet I could shoot his hat off his head without touchin' him if I'd got my catapult here," said William, in order to divert the limelight from Henry's intellect to his own physical prowess.

"Bet you couldn't," challenged Ginger.

"Bet I could," said William.

"Bet you couldn't."

"Bet I could."

It was the sort of discussion that can go on for ever. However, when it had gone only about ten minutes, William said with an air of finality:

"Well, I haven't got my catapult, anyway, or else I'd jolly well *show* you."

Ginger unexpectedly produced a catapult.

"Here's mine," he said.

"Well, I haven't got anything to shoot."

Douglas searched in his pocket and produced from beneath the inevitable string, hairy boiled sweets, penknife and piece of putty, two or three shrivelled peas.

William was taken aback till he realised that the Great Man had passed out of sight. Then he said, with something of relief: "Well, I can't, can I? Considerin' he's gone!" and added with withering sarcasm, "if you'll kin'ly tell me how to shoot the hat off a person's head what isn't here I'll be very glad to—"

But at that moment the figure of the Great Man was seen returning down the lane. He had only been to the post. The spirit of adventure – that Will-o'-the-wisp that had so often led the Outlaws astray but that they never could resist – entered into them.

"Go on, William," urged Ginger. "Have a shot at his hat an' see if you c'n knock it off. It won't matter. It'll only go 'ping' against his hat and we'll be across the next field before he knows what's happened. He'll never know it was us. Go on, William. Have a shot at his hat."

The figure was abreast of them now on the other side of the hedge.

William, his eyes gleaming with excitement, his face set and stern with determination, raised the catapult and had a shot at the Great Man's hat.

He had been unduly optimistic. He did not shoot the little hat off the Great Man's head as he had boasted he could. Instead he caught the Great Man himself just above his ear. It was, on the whole, not a very bad shot, but William did not stop to point that out to his friends. A dried pea emitted from a catapult can hurt more than those who have never received it have any conception of.

For a minute the Great Man was literally paralysed by the shock. Then he uttered a roar of pain, fury and outraged dignity and started forward, lusting for the blood of his assailant. The dastardly attack had seemed to come from the direction of the hedge. He flung himself in that direction. He could see three boys fleeing over the field and then – clutching desperately at the hedge above him – a fourth boy rolled back into the ditch. The Great Man pounced upon him. It was William, who had caught his foot while scrambling through the hedge, and lost his balance. He bore in his hand the evidence of his guilt in the shape of Ginger's catapult. It was useless for him to deny that he was the perpetrator of the outrage – useless even to plead the analogy of William Tell and the apple.

The Great Man had mastered the first violence of his fury. With a great effort he choked back several expressions which, though forcible, were unsuited for the ears of the young, and fixing William with a stern eye said severely: "I see by your cap that you attend the school at which I am to lecture tomorrow. After this outrage I shall not, of course, ask for the usual half-holiday, and I shall request your headmaster to inform your school-fellows of the reason why no half-holiday is accorded this year."

Then – stern, dignified, an impressive figure were it not for the smallness of his hat, which the shock of William's attack had further knocked slightly crooked – the Great Man passed down the lane.

William, with pale, set face, returned to his waiting friends.

"*Well!*" he said succinctly, "that's done it. That's jolly well *done* it." Then, savagely, to Ginger: "It's all your fault, taking your silly ole catapult about with you wherever you go an' gettin' people to shoot at other people all over the place. *Now* look what you've done."

"Huh! I like that!" said Ginger with spirit. "I like that. What about *you* falling about in ditches? If *you'd* not gone fallin' about in ditches he'd never've known about it. Huh! A nice Red Indian *you'd* make fallin' about in ditches. An', anyway, you were wrong an' I was right.

You *couldn't* shoot his hat off without touchin' his face. I *said* you couldn't."

He ended on a high-pitched note of jeering triumph which the proud spirit of William found intolerable. They hurled themselves upon each other in deadly combat, which was, however, terminated by Henry who enquired with innocent curiosity:

"What did he say, anyway?"

This suddenly reminded William of what the Great Man had said, and his fighting spirit died abruptly.

He sat down on the ground with Ginger on top of him and told them forlornly what the Great Man had said.

On hearing it Ginger's fighting spirit, too, died, and he got off William and sat in the road beside him.

"*Crumbs!*" he said in an awestruck voice of horror.

It was characteristic of the Outlaws that all their mutual recrimination promptly ceased at this news.

This was no mere misfortune. This was tragedy, and a tragedy in which they must all stand together. In the persecution from all ranks of their schoolfellows that would inevitably follow, they must identify themselves with William, their leader; they must share with him the ostracism, and worse than ostracism, that the Great Man's sentence would bring upon them.

"*Crumbs!*" breathed Henry, voicing their feelings, "won't they just be *mad!*"

"I'll tell 'em I did it," said William in a faint voice.

"You didn't do it," said Ginger aggressively. "Whose catapult was it, anyway? An' who dared you to?"

"An' whose pea was it?" put in Douglas with equal indignation.

"I did it, anyway," said William. "It was my fault. I'll tell 'em so."

"It was me just as much as you," said Ginger with spirit.

"It wasn't."

"It was."

"It wasn't."

"It was."

"It wasn't."

This argument, like the previous one, might have developed into a healthy physical contest had not Henry said slowly:

"He can't 've told *him* yet 'cause *he's* gone up to London to choose prizes an' I heard someone say he wun't be back till the last train tonight."

There was a silence. Through four grimy, freckled, disconsolate faces shone four sudden gleams of hope.

"P'raps if you told him you were sorry an' ask him not to—" suggested Douglas.

William leapt to his feet with alacrity.

"Come on," he said tersely and followed by his faithful band made his way across the field through the hedge and down the lane that led to the headmaster's house.

He performed an imperious and very lengthy tattoo on the knocker – a tattoo meant to be indicative of the strength and durability of his repentance.

A pretty housemaid appeared.

She saw one small and very dirty boy on the doorstep and three other small and very dirty boys hanging over the gate. She eyed them with disfavour. She disliked small and dirty boys.

"We're not deaf," she said haughtily.

"Aren't you?" said William with polite interest. "I'm not either. But I've gotter naunt what's so deaf that—"

"What do you want?" she snapped.

William, pulled up in this pleasant chat with the pretty housemaid, remembered what he wanted and said gloomily: "I want to speak to the man what's staying with the headmaster."

"What's your name?"

"William Brown."

"Well, stay there, and I'll ask him."

"All right," said William preparing to enter.

She pushed him back.

"I'm not having them boots in my hall," she said with passionate indignation, and went in, closing the door upon him.

William looked down at his boots with a puzzled frown and then called anxiously to his friends over the gate:

"There's nothing wrong with my boots, is there?"

They looked at William's boots, large, familiar, mud-encrusted.

"No," they said, "they're quite all right."

"What's she talkin' about, then?" said William.

"P'raps she means they're *muddy*," suggested Douglas tentatively.

"Well, that's what boots are *for*, i'n't it?" said William sternly.

Just then the housemaid returned and opened the door.

"He says if you're the boy who's just shot a catapult at him, certainly not."

It was quite obvious from William's expression that he *was* the boy.

"Well, what I wanted to say was that—"

Slowly but very firmly she was closing the door upon him. William planted one of his boots in the track of the closing door.

"Look here!" he said desperately, "tell him he can shoot a catapult at me. I don't mind. Look here. Tell him I'll put an apple on my head, an' he can—"

Again the housemaid indignantly pushed him back.

"Look at my *step!*" she said fiercely as she closed the door. "*You* and your *boots!*"

The door was quite closed now.

William opened the flap of the letter-box with his hand and said hoarsely:

"Tell him that it was all because of his hat. Say that—"

But she'd disappeared and it was obvious that she didn't intend to return.

He rejoined his friends at the gate.

"'S no good," he said dejectedly. "She won't even listen to me. Jus' keeps on talkin' about my boots. They're jus' the same as anyone else's boots, as far as I can see. Anyway, what're we goin' to do now?"

"Let's find out what he's doin' tonight," said Ginger. "If he's goin' anywhere you might meet him on the way an' see if he'll listen to you."

"Yes," said William, "that's a jolly good idea, but – how're we goin' to find out what he's doin' tonight?"

"It's after tea-time," announced Henry rather patheti-cally. (Henry hated missing his meals.) "I votes we go

WILLIAM PLANTED HIS FOOT IN THE TRACK OF THE CLOSING
DOOR. "LOOK HERE!" HE SAID DESPERATELY. "TELL HIM HE
CAN SHOOT A CATAPULT AT ME. I DON'T MIND!"

home to tea now and then come back an' talk it over some more."

"I shouldn't be surprised if it's goin' to be rather hard," said William still dejectedly, "findin' out what he's goin' to do tonight."

But it turned out to be quite simple.

While Douglas was having tea he heard his father say to his mother that he'd heard that the headmaster's cousin was going to dine with the Carroways, as the headmaster had gone to London on business and wasn't coming back till the last train.

Douglas joyfully took this news back to the meeting of the Outlaws.

They gave him a hearty cheer and William began to look as if the whole thing was now settled.

"*That's* all right," he said. "Now I'll go 'n' stay by the front gate of the Carroway house till he comes along and then I'll plead with him."

They looked at him rather doubtfully. Somehow they couldn't visualise William pleading. William defying, William commanding, were familiar figures, but they had never yet seen William pleading.

"We'll come along with you," said Ginger, "an' help you."

"All right," said William cheerfully. "We'll all plead. It oughter melt him all right, *four* people pleadin'. What time ought we to be there?"

"I 'spect they have dinner at half-past seven," said Ginger.

"Let's be there at quarter past six so's to be quite sure not to miss him."

*

They reached the Carroways' at a quarter past six and took up their posts by the gate. So far, so good. All would, in fact, have gone splendidly had not a circus happened to be in the act of unloading itself in the field next to the Carroways' house. The Outlaws caught a glimpse of tents, vans, cages. They heard the sound of a muffled roar, they distinctly saw an elephant. It was more than flesh and blood could stand.

"Well," said William carelessly, "we've got here too early an' it's no good wastin' time hangin' about. Let's jus' go'n wait in the field jus' for five minutes or so. That can't do any harm."

Douglas, who was of a cautious disposition, demurred, but his protests were half-hearted and already the others were through the hedge and making their way to the little crowd that surrounded the caravans and cages. It was beyond their wildest dreams. There was a lion. There was a tiger. There was an elephant. There was a bear. There were several monkeys. They saw a monkey bite a piece out of someone's trousers. William laughed at this so much that they thought he was going to be sick. The bear sat on its hind legs and flapped its arms. The lion roared. The elephant took someone's hat off. The whole thing was beyond description.

The Outlaws wandered about, getting in everyone's way, putting their noses through the bars of every cage, miraculously escaping sudden death at every turn. It was when William thought that they must have been there nearly five minutes that they asked the time and found that it was twenty past seven. They had been there over an hour.

"*Crumbs!*" they ejaculated in dismay, and William said slowly:

"Seems impossible to me. P'raps," with sudden hope, "their clocks are wrong."

But their clocks weren't wrong. They asked four or five other men and were impatiently given the same reply.

Aghast, they wandered back to the gate where they had meant to accost the Great Man, but they realised that it was no use waiting there now. He would certainly have arrived by now.

"Let's go up the drive," said Ginger, "an' see if we c'n see him."

They crept up the drive. Dusk was falling quickly and the downstairs rooms were lit up. The drawing-room curtains were not drawn and the Outlaws were rewarded by the sight of the Great Man standing on the hearth-rug talking to Mr and Mrs Carroway.

They stared at him forlornly from the bushes.

"*Well!*" moaned William, "of all the *rotten* luck!"

Then they discussed the crisis in hoarse whispers. It would be impossible, of course, to wait till he came home and by tomorrow he would have seen and reported matters to the headmaster. Anyone less determined than the Outlaws would have abandoned the project and gone home. But not the Outlaws.

"Let's go round to the other side of the house," said William, "an' have a look at the dining-room. We might get a chance to whisper to him through the window or somethin'."

This was felt to be unduly optimistic, but the suggestion appealed to the Outlaws' spirit of adventure and they followed William round to the side of the house.

The dining-room window was open but the curtains were drawn. The curtains, however, did not quite meet at the top and William said that by climbing on to the roof of the summer-house he thought he could see into the room.

Using Ginger and Douglas as a step ladder, he hoisted himself up on to the roof of the summer-house. It was now so dark that he could not see the Outlaws down among the bushes.

"I can't see into the room yet," he whispered, "but," he added optimistically, "I bet if I stand on tiptoe—"

At this point the Outlaws became conscious of some sort of a commotion, of the sound of many excited voices. Then a man with a lighted lantern began to make what was obviously a tour of inspection of the garden.

William crouched down upon his summer-house and the others crouched down among the bushes.

The man with the lighted lantern passed, muttering to himself.

The Great Man stood in the drawing-room talking to Mr and Mrs Carroway and to Mrs Carroway's companion, Miss Seed.

It was, of course, unfortunate that Mrs Carroway's companion was called Miss Seed, and had there been any other suitable applicant for the post Mrs Carroway would certainly not have chosen Miss Seed. However, there hadn't been, so both of them made the best of the situation and had brought to a fine art the capacity of looking quite unconscious when their names were pronounced together.

The Great Man was talking. The Great Man was, as a matter of fact, never completely happy unless he was talking, and he had been pleased to find that he was the only guest because he so often found that other guests liked to talk as well, and that completely spoilt the evening for him. He was, however, rather annoyed when Mrs Carroway was called out to someone at the front door in the middle of his very brilliant summary of the political situation. He cleared his throat in an annoyed fashion, frowned, and stood in silence watching the door for her return. He didn't consider Mr Carroway alone worth addressing, and Miss Seed had gone out to see to the dinner, because Mrs Carroway was, as usual, without maids and one of the reasons why Mrs Carroway had chosen Miss Seed as a companion, despite her name, was that she did not mind seeing to dinners in the intervals of companioning Mrs Carroway. After a few minutes Mrs Carroway returned.

"When I say that this Government has missed some of its finest opportunities," he began at once, "I refer of course—"

But Mrs Carroway didn't wait to hear to what he referred. She didn't care at all what opportunities the Government had missed.

"What *shall* we do?" she burst out hysterically. "Here's a man to say that a lion has escaped from the circus and they think it may be in our back garden, because there's only a fence between our back garden and the field where the circus is. Oh, what *shall* we do? We shall all be eaten alive."

The Great Man cleared his throat and took command of the situation.

109

"Send the man round the garden to search," he said, "and we will meantime remain perfectly calm and lock up all the doors and windows. Be brave, Mrs Carroway, and trust yourself to my protection. I will see that all the doors and windows are securely fastened. Courage! Remember we are English men and, ahem, English women, and must show no fear. Lock and bolt the front door at once and shout through the letter-box to the man to make a thorough search of the garden."

This was done. The man seemed slightly peeved and went off alone muttering.

The Great Man then made a tour of the house, closing every door and window firmly. Finally, he collected Mr and Mrs Carroway and Miss Seed into the drawing-room where he locked the shutters and moved the grand piano across the door.

"Let courage and fortitude be our motto," he said. "Let us now meet danger calmly."

No one listened to him. Miss Seed was tending Mrs Carroway who was in hysterics and was hoping that she'd soon be sufficiently recovered to allow her to have them in her turn, and Mr Carroway was trying to get under the sofa.

The Great Man, therefore, had no one to address but his own reflection in the full-length mirror. So he addressed it spiritedly.

"England expects—" he began. At this moment there came a loud rat-tat-tat at the knocker. Mrs Carroway, who was just coming out of hysterics, went into them again, and Mr Carroway put his head out of the sofa to say reassuringly: "Don't be alarmed, dearest. It can't be the lion. The lion couldn't reach up to the knocker."

Then someone pushed open the letter-box and the voice of the man with the lantern called: "He ain't in your garden, mister. I've been all over your garden," and added sarcastically: "You can come out from hunder the sofa. 'E won't 'urt you."

"What a very impertinent man," said Mr Carroway. "I shall report him to the manager of his firm."

The Great Man began to unbarricade the door.

"We may all justly pride ourselves," he said, "upon the dauntless courage we have displayed in face of this crisis."

"I'm so hungry," said Miss Seed pathetically.

"Hungry?" said Mrs Carroway. "I'm *past* hunger. I shall never, never, *never* be able to describe to you what I've suffered during these last few minutes."

Mr Carroway looked rather relieved at the information.

They went into the dining-room and took their seats. Miss Seed brought in the dinner, and the Great Man returned to the opportunities the Government had missed.

"I still feel faint," said Mrs Carroway, unwilling to share the limelight with the government or anyone else. "I still feel most faint. I always do after any nervous shock."

Her husband went to the window and drew back the curtains and opened the window.

"I – I don't know that I'd do that," said Mrs Carroway, gazing fearfully out into the dark garden. "One can't be *quite* sure – I mean—"

At that moment came the sound of a heavy body crashing through the undergrowth. With a wild scream Mrs Carroway rose and fled from the room.

MR CARROWAY CRAWLED OUT FROM UNDER THE SOFA.

THE GREAT MAN BEGAN TO UNBARRICADE THE DOOR. "WE MAY
ALL JUSTLY PRIDE OURSELVES," HE SAID, "UPON OUR
DAUNTLESS COURAGE!"

"Quick," she panted, "out of the front door and across
to the Vicarage for refuge. The creature is gathering for
a spring. This house is unsafe—"

She was half-way down the front drive by this time,
followed closely by the others. The Great Man, being far
from nimble on his feet, panted along at the end, gasping,
"Courage, friends . . . let courage be our motto."

The house was left empty and silent.

*

The sound of the heavy crashing through the undergrowth had of course been William leaping down from the roof of the shed to join his companions below, losing his balance just as he leapt, and falling among the laurel bushes.

He sat up, rubbing his head and ejecting laurel leaves from his mouth. Then: "I say, what's all the fuss about?" he whispered. "I thought I heard someone scream."

"So'd I," said the Outlaws mystified.

"What was that man goin' round with a lantern for?" whispered William.

"I d'no," said the Outlaws, still more mystified.

"Well," said William, abandoning the mystery for the moment, "let's go an' see if we can see what they're doin' now. Someone's drawn the curtains."

They crept up through the bushes to the open dining-room window. To their amazement they saw a brightly lit room, a table laid for four, steaming dishes upon it, and chairs drawn up in position – all completely empty.

"Crumbs!" said William in amazement, "that's queer."

The Outlaws gazed in silence at the astounding sight till Ginger said weakly:

"Where've they all *gone* to?"

"P'raps they're in the other room," suggested Douglas.

They crept round to the drawing-room window. The drawing-room was empty.

"P'raps – p'raps," said Henry without conviction, "they're all in the kitchen."

They crept round to the kitchen. The kitchen was

empty. They looked at the upstairs windows. They were all in darkness.

William scratched his head and frowned.

"'S very mysterious," he commented.

Then they returned to the dining-room. It was still empty. The steaming dishes were still upon the table. An odour was wafted out to the waiting Outlaws – an odour so succulent that it was impossible to resist it. It was William who first swung himself over the low window sill of the open window into the room. The others followed. They stood in silence and gazed at the steaming dishes on the table, the four places, the four chairs.

"Seems," said Ginger dreamily, "seems sort of like a fairy-tale – like a sort of Arabian Nights story."

"Well," said William slowly, "it cert'nly seems sort of *meant*."

"I read a tale once like this," said Douglas, "and they sat down at the table and invisible hands waited on them."

"Let's try," said William suddenly, taking his seat at the head of the table, "let's try if invisible hands'll wait on us."

They needed no encouragement. They all took their seats with alacrity. In fairness to whatever invisible hands might have waited upon the Outlaws, it must be admitted that they did not get much chance. The Outlaws began immediately to wait upon themselves with visible and very grimy hands. Each had a suspicion that at any minute the feast might be interrupted. None of them really had much faith in the Arabian Nights idea. Under the cover in front of William was a roast chicken. The dishes contained bread sauce, gravy, potatoes and cauliflower. William dismembered the chicken ruthlessly and with a fine disregard for anatomy, and they helped themselves from the various dishes. It was a glorious meal. There was in the room complete silence, broken only by the sounds of the Outlaws endeavouring to put away as much of this gorgeous repast as they could before the dream should fade into reality, and some grown-up confront them, demanding explanation. They did not draw breath till every dish was bare and then, flushed and panting, they sat back and William said meditatively: "Wonder what they were goin' to have after this?"

Douglas suggested giving the invisible hands a chance, but the suggestion was not popular and Henry, catching sight of a hatch in the wall, went to investigate. The hatch slid up and on the ledge just inside was waiting a magnificent cream edifice and a little pile of four plates. Four gasps of ecstasy went up. Again there was silence, broken only by the sounds of the Outlaws working hard against time. At last that dish, too, was empty. There was a barrel of biscuits and a pile of fruit on the sideboard, but the capacity even of the Outlaws was exhausted.

"I feel I wouldn't want to eat another thing for hundreds and hundreds of years," said Henry blissfully.

"Seems about time we woke up now," said Douglas.

But to William, who lived ever in the present, the feast, though the most gorgeous of its kind he had ever known, was already a thing of the past, and he was concentrating his whole attention on the problem of the present.

"I wonder what's *happened* to 'em?" he said. "I wonder where they *are*."

"Looks like the thing old Markie was tellin' us about in school yesterday," said Henry, "a place where a volcano went off suddenly, an' killed all the people and left their houses an' furniture an' things an' you can see it today. It's called Pomples or somethin' like that."

This information as emanating from Authority and savouring of swank was rightly ignored.

"P'raps they've all died suddenly of the plague or something," suggested Douglas cheerfully.

But the best suggestion came from Ginger.

"I guess someone's murdered them an' hid all their dead bodies upstairs. I bet if we go upstairs we'll find all their dead bodies hid there."

Much inspirited at this prospect the Outlaws swarmed upstairs and concluded a thorough search of the premises. The search was disappointing.

"Not many dead bodies," said William rather bitterly.

Ginger, feeling that his prestige had suffered from his failure to prove his theory, looked about him and with a yell of glee, said:

"No, but look! There's a trap-door up there and I bet we could get out on to the roof from it."

The Outlaws completely forgot both feast and dead bodies in the thrill of the trap-door by which you could get out on to the roof.

"Who'll try it first?" said William.

"Bags me. I saw it first," said Ginger.

He climbed on to the balusters, leapt at the trap-door, caught it by a miracle, and swung himself up. It was a spectacle guaranteed to give any mother nervous break-downs for months.

"Does it go out on to the roof?" called the Outlaws, breathless with suspense.

Faint but ecstatic came back Ginger's voice:

"Yes, it does. It's scrummy. Right on the edge of the roof. I can see right down into the garden. I can—"

"Shut up," hissed William, "someone's coming."

Downstairs Mr and Mrs Carroway, Miss Seed and the Great Man entered the hall and hastily shut and locked the front door.

They had gone to the Vicarage and stayed there for an hour. To the Vicar and his wife it had seemed much more than an hour because Mrs Carroway was acquiring a fatal facility in hysterics and was apparently beginning to count every moment wasted that was not devoted to them.

Finally the Vicar rang up the police, learnt that the missing lion had been seen going down the road at the other end of the village, and politely but firmly insisted on his guests departing homewards. He was beginning to fear the effect of Mrs. Carroway's hysterics upon his wife. No woman likes being put so completely in the shade as Mrs Carroway's hysterics put the Vicar's wife, and he had noticed that she was beginning to watch the various stages of the attacks with an interest that suggested to him that she was storing them up for future use.

"Nothing," wailed Mrs Carroway, "*nothing* will induce me to leave this house again tonight. What I have suffered during that terrible walk from the Vicarage, hearing and seeing lions at every step, no one will ever understand. *No* one. If I talked all night I couldn't make you understand."

"I'm sure you couldn't, dear," said her husband hastily.

"I – er – I suppose the house *is* safe," said the Great

Man uneasily. "I – er – I cannot help remembering that we left the – er – the dining-room window open and that the – er – the place from which the – er – the beast escaped was – er – just over the fence."

"Miss Seed," said Mrs Carroway faintly, "go and see whether there are any traces of it in the dining-room. The food, you remember, was left on the table. If that has been tampered with—"

Miss Seed sidled cautiously to the dining-room and peeped in. Then she gave a wild scream.

"It's been here," she panted. "It's been here. It's been here. It's eaten up everything. It must be in the house – NOW!"

Miss Seed, of course, was overwrought, or she would have stopped to take into consideration the fact that a lion does not eat out of a plate with knives and forks and spoons and that even if it did one lion would not have used four of each.

"It must be in the house NOW!" she repeated desperately.

There was a sudden silence – a silence of paralysed horror. Through this silence came the sound of a heavy crash upstairs, followed by a snarl of rage.

In less time than it takes to tell the hall was empty.

Mrs Carroway had locked herself into the conservatory.

Miss Seed was under the drawing-room sofa.

Mr Carroway was on the drawing-room mantelpiece.

The Great Man was in the rug-box in the hall.

The heavy crash had been Ginger overbalancing and falling back through the trap-door upon William in his over-anxiety to find out what was going on. The snarl of rage was William's involuntary reaction to the sudden descent of Ginger's solid form upon him.

The Outlaws, aghast at the noise they had made, froze into a petrified silence.

The four grown-ups, in their hiding-places downstairs, also froze in a petrified silence.

Complete silence reigned throughout the house.

The minutes passed slowly by – one minute, two minutes, three minutes, five minutes. Of the eight people in the house no one spoke, no one moved, no one breathed.

At last William whispered: "They must've gone out again."

"I din't hear the door," hissed Ginger.

"I'm goin' to see," said William.

He peeped cautiously over the balusters. The hall was empty. The only sound was the solemn ticking of the grandfather clock.

"I b'lieve they *have* gone out again," whispered William. "I'm goin' down. Seems to me they're all potty."

He took off his shoes, crept silently down the stairs to the empty, silent hall and stood there irresolute.

Then he thought he heard a movement in a chest near the clock. He approached it and listened. Heavy, raucous breathing came from inside. He raised the lid. As he did so there came from it a high-pitched scream of terror. The open lid revealed the Great Man. The high-pitched scream of terror had come from the Great Man. William stared at him in blank amazement.

The Great Man, instead of seeing the fanged, tawny face he had expected when the chest lid began slowly to open, met the astonished gaze of the boy who had shot at him with a catapult that morning.

They stared at each other in silence. Then a thoughtful expression came over the face of the Great Man.

"Er – was it you who made that noise upstairs?" he said.

WILLIAM AND THE GREAT MAN STARED BLANKLY AT EACH OTHER. "ER – WAS IT YOU WHO MADE THAT NOISE UPSTAIRS?" THE GREAT MAN ASKED.

"Yes," said William. "Ginger fell on me. I bet you'd've made a noise if Ginger'd fell on you."

The expression of the Great Man became yet more thoughtful.

"And the – er – the dinner—?" he said, still reclining in the rug-box.

"Yes," admitted William, "it – it seemed sort of *meant*."

Slowly, stiffly, the Great Man climbed out of the rug-box. It had been a very tight fit.

Just then the telephone bell rang, and the Great Man went to answer it. He was glad of the diversion. He was remembering more and more clearly the high-pitched cry of terror he had uttered as the chest opened. He was wondering what explanation he could give this boy of that and of his presence in the rug-box.

The telephone call was from the police. The lion had been found. The rumour that it had been seen at the other end of the village had proved to be incorrect. On escaping from its cage it had wandered into the further field and gone to sleep in the shelter of a hayrick. It had just been discovered, roused and taken back to its cage.

Within a few minutes Miss Seed was putting Mrs Carroway to bed, Mr Carroway was trying to mend the more valuable of the ornaments he had displaced from the mantelpiece in his hurried ascent, and the Great Man had called William aside. The Great Man was aware that this was a situation requiring delicate handling. He had tried to think of some dignified explanation of his presence in the rug-box and of that unfortunate scream, and not one had occurred to him. He had decided, therefore, not to attempt any. Instead he assumed his most genial expression and said:

"I believe, my boy, that you – er – are the boy who accidentally – er – hit me with some missile this morning."

"Yes," said William simply, "a pea."

"I have no doubt at all," said the Great Man, "that it was – er – an accident, and – ahem – I do not after all intend to mention the matter to your headmaster."

"Thank you," said William, but without much enthusiasm. William knew when he held the reins of a situation in his hand.

The Great Man continued: "No need for you – ahem – for you to mention to anyone what has occurred here tonight."

William said nothing. His face was drained of expression. His eye was blank.

"I will, of course," went on the Great Man hastily, "I will – ahem – of course ask for the usual half-holiday from your headmaster."

William turned upon the Great Man his expressionless face and his blank eye and said suavely:

"Why not ask for two, sir?"

The Great Man swallowed and cleared his throat. Then, with a more or less convincing attempt at heartiness, he said: "Certainly, my boy. Certainly. A very good idea. I'll ask for two. And with regard to what happened here tonight—"

The Great Man was uncomfortably aware that the story of what had happened there that night as told by this boy might take some living down.

But William's face was still expressionless, his eye still blank.

"You hidin' in that box to give me a fright?" he said carelessly. "Oh, no! Why, I've nearly forgot that already." His blank, unblinking eye was fixed upon the Great Man. "I bet that after two half-holidays I'll have forgot it altogether."

The Great Man brought out the request for two half-holidays with something of an effort. The headmaster wasn't prepared for it and was taken aback. However, he didn't want to offend the Great Man, so after a brief inward struggle he promised the two half-holidays.

Frenzied cheers rent the air.

At the back of the hall, in the back row, sat William nonchalantly manufacturing a blotting-paper dart, wholly unmoved apparently by the glorious news.

"Din't you hear?" yelled a frenzied neighbour, "din't you *hear? Two* half-holidays."

"Yes, I heard all right," said William carelessly.

And, making careful aim, threw his dart at Ginger.

CHAPTER SIX

WILLIAM AND THE TEMPORARY HISTORY MASTER

WILLIAM HAD THOUGHT that school could not possibly be worse than it was, but quite suddenly – half-way through the term – he discovered his mistake. The history master, a mild and elderly man, conveniently short-sighted, conveniently deaf, and still more conveniently fond of expounding his own historical theories without in the least minding whether anyone listened to them or not, caught scarlet fever and was removed to hospital.

For a few glorious lessons William's form spent the history hour officially doing homework, but in reality indulging in such sports and pastimes as dart throwing, earwig racing, ruler-and-rubber cricket, and ink slinging. Then the "temporary" arrived – a small, smug man with protruding teeth and a manner that hovered between the hearty, the jocular, and the sarcastic. He had, moreover, modern theories about the teaching of history. He believed in making it real by acting it. When he gave a lesson on the Magna Charta one of the boys had to be King John and the others the turbulent barons. When he gave a lesson on Charles I, one of them had to be Charles I, and another the executioner, and so on. The novelty of this proceeding had long worn off as far as Mr Renies himself was concerned, and he now relieved the monotony of it as far as possible by choosing for the principal and most dramatic parts boys who were obviously devoid of histrionic talent. This enabled him to make clever little jibes at their clumsiness, jibes that were always rewarded by the sycophantic titters of the other boys. Mr Renies loved these sycophantic titters. He didn't consider them sycophantic, of course. He considered them honest tributes to his sparkling wit and brilliant flashes of humour. Mr Renies, it is perhaps unnecessary to add, thought a great deal of himself, more in fact than most other people thought of him. He was certainly clever in picking out the right boy for his butt – self-conscious, inarticulate, and yet not insensitive.

On the first day on which Mr Renies faced William's form he looked round for his butt and his eye fell on William. William, it must be admitted, looked the part to perfection.

"What's your name?" said Mr Renies.

"Brown," admitted William suspiciously.

Mr Renies' face beamed with anticipatory pleasure.

"Well, Brown," he said kindly, "suppose you come out here and give us your idea of Charles the First before the House of Commons demanding the arrest of the five members . . ."

Alone or with his Outlaws William could act the hero in the most stirring scenes that the imagination could possibly conceive, but to be ordered to act as part of a lesson by this objectionable little man was quite another

RELUCTANTLY WILLIAM CAME UP TO THE FRONT OF THE CLASS.
THERE HE STOOD, PURPLE WITH ANGER AND EMBARRASSMENT,
GLARING FEROCIOUSLY AT THE MASTER.

thing. Reluctantly he came up to the front of the class. There he stood, purple-faced with anger and embarrassment, glaring ferociously at Mr Renies and the class. Mr Renies' smile broadened. He enlivened the lesson with frequent references to "this kingly figure" ... "this mien of majesty", and was rewarded as usual by a chorus of titters from boys who were relieved that his choice had fallen on William and not on them.

The next day he ordered William to impersonate Prince Rupert and the day after that Oliver Cromwell. William impersonated both by the simple means of staring furiously and doggedly in front of him, and Mr Renies' enjoyment increased.

He referred to him as "this noble youth", "this valiant hero", and even as "this spirited young actor".

William disliked it, but saw no other course than to endure it. He had no weapon against Mr Renies except in his imagination, and he worked his imagination very hard during those days. There had been a side show in the last fair that had visited the village called "Picture of 200 different forms of Torture". and William had paid his 1*d*. entrance fee and spent an enthralled half-hour in the tent. He now put Mr Renies in imagination through every one of the two hundred forms of torture. As Mr Renies, gay and debonair, stood at his desk and poured forth his stream of little witticisms, he had no idea of course that William saw him writhing on a rack or struggling in boiling oil. In fact so horrible and so real were these pictures to William that he couldn't help feeling that he had scored. After all, what was being made to feel a fool before the class in comparison with being impaled on spikes and rolled down-hill in a barrel full of nails – things that happened to Mr Renies several times an hour? But even Mr Renies could go too far.

"Now, Brown," he said, with his toothy smile, "we must think out a nice part for you for next revision lesson. How about" – he rose to dazzling heights of wit – "making you Henrietta Maria and I'll be Buckingham and come to woo you? That would be nice, boys, wouldn't it?" The bored titter that Mr Renies looked upon as a spontaneous tribute to his wit broke out again dutifully, and Mr Renies continued: "Our young actor doesn't look pleased . . . You must come round to my house some evening, my friend, and we'll practise some of these rôles together."

William began to be dimly aware that this state of things could not go on, and that something must be done about it, but it was a quite justifiable action on the part of Mr Renies that finally roused him.

Mr Renies was in the habit of confiscating any article with which he saw his pupils playing, and, finding William opening the back of his watch and trying to replace a little wheel that he had taken out to sharpen a pencil point, he confiscated it. The watch had not been going for some weeks, and in any case William never cared what time it was, so it cannot be said that the loss of the watch as a means of telling the time seriously inconvenienced him. In fact, if his mother had not had a letter from the aunt who had given him the watch, saying that she was coming to see them the next week and adding facetiously that she need not bring her grandfather clock because William would be able to tell her the time by his nice new watch, William would never have thought of it again. The fact that the watch wasn't going wouldn't matter, of course. His aunt, aware that it was a cheap watch and unaware that William took from it regularly any of its component parts that he needed for his various experiments (such as making a motor-launch, or a treadwheel for his pet stag beetle), would merely have offered to pay for it being mended, as she had already done once or twice. But the fact that it had passed out of his possession entirely would matter a great deal. Aunts are notoriously touchy on such points, and it would probably matter so much that she would not give him the customary tip on her departure. Therefore William decided by hook or by crook to recover his watch. He gave Mr Renies the chance of acting magnanimously by asking for it. He asked for it when Mr Renies was alone in the form room, and, as there was no appreciative audience to render him its homage of titters, Mr Renies wasted none of his famous wit on William, but merely snapped "Certainly not!"

Therefore no course was left to William, as William saw the situation, but that of entering Mr Renies' house, where presumably Mr Renies kept his ill-gotten gains, and taking the watch from Mr Renies as lawlessly as, William considered, Mr Renies had taken it from him.

And so the night before his aunt's visit William approached the history master's house (where Mr Renies was temporarily domiciled), having left Mr Renies in his form room correcting exercises.

He knocked boldly at the front door. A maid wearing a grimy apron and a dreamy expression came to answer his knock.

"I've called with a message from Mr Renies," said William, meeting her eye squarely, "he says you needn't stop in any longer this evening. You can go out now."

The maid, fortunately for William, was of a simple and credulous disposition. Moreover she was in love. To go out meant meeting the beloved, therefore she was willing to believe implicitly any message that told her to go out.

"What about his supper?" she said.

"Oh, he won't be a minute," said William reassuringly. "He says just leave it ready."

"What about locking up?" said the maid, who was already in imagination walking down a country lane clasped tightly in the stalwart arm of the beloved.

"He says put the key on the window-sill," said William.

A few minutes later the maid laid the key upon the window-sill and flew on winged feet to Paradise and the beloved.

A few minutes later still William took the key from the window-sill and opened the front door.

Mr Renies walked slowly up to his house. He felt pleased with the world in general and himself in particular. He had finished his corrections early, he had got some good fun out of that kid – what was his name – Brown – he was going home to a delicious supper of pheasant, bread sauce, baked potatoes, brussels sprouts, followed by a pineapple cream and a savoury. Mr Renies liked to do himself well, but it wasn't often that he could rise to such heights as this. The supper was in honour of the pheasant that had been sent to him by a cousin who was staying at a "shoot". Mr Renies had been looking forward to it all day.

He opened his front door and stood for a minute in the hall, dilating his nostrils and drawing in the delicious odour with an anticipatory smile. Then he hung up his hat, washed his hands, called out: "I'm ready, Ellen," and went toward the dining-room, rubbing his hands, and smacking his lips. He flung open the door and entered. And there the first shock awaited him. Upon the table stood a dish containing the well-picked carcase of a pheasant, flanked by empty vegetable dishes. At his place was an empty well-scraped plate that had recently contained pheasant, bread sauce, baked potatoes, gravy and brussels sprouts. On it were laid at an unconventional angle the knife and fork that had evidently been used in the consumption of the repast. There was an empty dish that had evidently once contained a pineapple cream and another dish that had evidently contained a savoury. For a moment Mr Renies was literally paralysed with horror and amazement. His eyes grew fixed and glassy. His mouth dropped open. Then he cried: "Ellen!" and rushed to the kitchen. The kitchen was empty. Ellen's cap and apron were hung neatly behind the door. He called: "Ellen!" still more wildly, but no one answered. It was quite clear that Ellen was no longer in the house. Mr Renies dashed upstairs to his study. And there the second shock awaited him. The drawer in which he kept the articles that he confiscated in school was open and empty.

"Burglars!" was his first thought but he found on examination that nothing else in the room was missing. Then he heard a sound in the big cupboard by the window, and for a moment the wild idea flashed into his head that rats were responsible for everything – the eating of his supper, the emptying of the drawers and the strange noise in the cupboard. He remembered in time, however, that rats do not use knives and forks. He flung open the cupboard door and there he got his third shock. For William crouched in the cupboard blinking at him.

William had not really meant to eat Mr Renies' supper. He had peeped into the dining-room and found the meal laid there. It looked very appetising, and William was very hungry. William decided to eat a very little of it, so little that Mr Renies couldn't possibly notice. It wasn't till he discovered that he had eaten so much that Mr Renies couldn't possibly help noticing it, that he decided that he might as well finish it. So he finished it and thoroughly enjoyed it. It was, he decided, the best meal he'd ever had in his life (better even than Christmas dinner because there was no one there to worry him about manners), and worth any consequences. Then he went upstairs to find his watch. He found it quite easily in the first drawer he opened. With it were a penknife of Ginger's, a mouth organ of Douglas's, a catapult of Henry's and numerous other articles belonging to other boys. William decided that he might as well take them all. He would give their property back to Ginger and Henry and Douglas and sell the rest to their owners. William possessed a strong commercial instinct. Just as he was putting the last article (a pistol belonging to Smith minimus) into his pocket he heard someone enter the house. He stood still and listened. Soon there came a ferocious bellow, angry cries of "Ellen!" and the sound of heavy footsteps ascending the stairs. Without a moment's hesitation William flung himself into the only cupboard the room possessed and closed the doors. Unfortunately the cupboard was already full of other things than William, and William's figure, though small, was not the sort of figure to accommodate itself to the thin zig-zag line of space left between a pile of books, a duplicating machine, half a dozen croquet mallets, a dozen Indian clubs, an old-fashioned camera on a stand and a large moth-eaten stag's head with branching antlers. With great difficulty he took up a posture that was in the shape of the letter S, but one of the stag's antlers was digging so mercilessly into his neck that he moved slightly in order to relieve the pressure, and knocked over the pile of books. Almost immediately the cupboard door was flung open, and the amazed and furious face of Mr Renies appeared. William was glad to be saved from the murderous attack of the moth-eaten stag, but otherwise he realised that the situation was a delicate one. There was no doubt at all that Mr Renies was very angry. He dragged William out by his ear and thundered:

"What is the meaning of this?"

"WHAT IS THE MEANING OF THIS?" THUNDERED MR RENIES.

For a moment William was at a loss how to answer, then inspiration came to him. He assumed a vacant expression.

"Please, sir," he said, "you asked me to come to your house an' practise actin' history scenes some evening, so I came, an' I was jus' practis'n' bein' Charles the First in hidin' when you came in."

Mr Renies sputtered angrily. His eye fell upon the empty drawer.

"PLEASE, SIR," REPLIED WILLIAM, "YOU ASKED ME TO COME TO YOUR HOUSE AND PRACTISE ACTING HISTORY SCENES."

"And did you *dare*," he stormed, "to open a private drawer of mine and empty it?"

Inspiration again came to William. He realised with surprise that he knew more history than he had thought.

"No, sir," he said innocently, "I was practisin' being Jack Cade's rebellion lootin' and plunderin'."

Then the memory of the supreme outrage of that evening came back to Mr Renies, and for a minute his fury and anguish deprived him of the power of speech. Finally he stuttered:

"And – and – and – downstairs – was it *you* who *dared* to—"

William by now had his wits well about him.

"That?" he said. "Oh yes, sir. I was practisin' actin' that king that died of a surfeit of lampreys. I couldn't find any lampreys so I jus' had to eat what I could find. I didn't die of it either but that wasn't my fault."

With a howl of fury Mr Renies flung himself upon William, but William was already half-way downstairs.

"I'm practisin' bein' Charles II fleein' after the battle of Worcester," he called over his shoulder as he ran.

Mr Renies plunged downstairs after him. This was an occasion for immediate revenge. A man as deeply outraged in his dignity and his stomach as Mr Renies had been does not defer punishment till the next morning. The pleasant perfume of roast pheasant that hung about the hall increased his anger to the point of madness as he passed through it. In the dusk he could see the figure of William fleeing down the road. He followed, and fury lent wings to him. Fury, in fact, lent such wings that William began to feel slightly disconcerted. It is not easy to run really fast on such a meal as William had just partaken of, and there was no doubt that Mr Renies was gaining on him. That retribution must follow the evening's exploit sooner or later William was well aware, but he preferred it to be later rather than sooner. Certainly he didn't want to receive it at the hands of an enraged Mr Renies in the middle of the road. Mr Renies was a better runner than he looked, and slowly but steadily he was gaining on his quarry. It was too late now even to plunge through the hedge into a field. The time it would take to turn off from the road would deliver him into his enemy's hands. And William rightly judged that it would take more than a hedge to stop the raging pheasantless man behind him. He was quite near him now. Almost upon him. Only a miracle could save William. Turning a sharp bend in the road he ran into his sister, who was taking a leisurely walk with a girl friend. Nimbly William dodged aside and took cover behind them. Round the corner immediately after him came Mr Renies, his arms outstretched to catch that little fiend who was at last within his grasp. He collided violently with Ethel and her friend. He lost his balance and clung to them to save himself – an arm round the neck of each. From behind them came William's voice breathless but quite distinct.

"This is Mr Renies, Ethel," he said. "He's our history master. He goes about actin' history scenes. He's actin' " – the sight of Mr Renies, still clasping the necks of Ethel and her friend in an attempt to recover his balance, suggested an irresistible parallel – "he's actin' he's Henry the Eighth now," he ended and disappeared into the dusk.

He didn't disappear alone, however. Mr Renies, his fury again roused to boiling-point, dashed after him. William had had a slight start, but the added fury of Mr

Renies' spirit again seemed to give speed to his feet. Again he was on the point of catching William, when William suddenly darted through the open garden gate belonging to a house that bordered the road. William knew the garden well. There was a lily pond in the middle of the lawn. William sometimes took a forbidden short

NIMBLY WILLIAM DODGED ASIDE AND TOOK COVER BEHIND HIS
SISTER AND HER FRIEND.

cut through the garden and took the lily pond literally in his stride. He cleared it now with a skill born of long practice. Mr Renies was at a disadvantage. He didn't know that there was a lily pond and in the dusk he did not notice it. He followed William's flying figure and – found himself up to the shoulders in water. The sound of the splash and of the shout of anger and surprise that accompanied it, brought an elderly lady down from the

ROUND THE CORNER CAME MR RENIES, HIS ARMS OUTSTRETCHED TO CATCH THAT LITTLE FIEND WHO WAS AT LAST WITHIN HIS GRASP.

house to investigate. She found a man floundering in her lily pond and a boy standing by the side watching him.

"What on earth does this mean?" asked the lady majestically.

Mr Renies tried to explain, but he couldn't, because he'd swallowed a pint of water and several lily buds in his sudden descent.

"Is he drunk?" went on the lady.

"No," said William, "he's not exactly drunk. He's Mr Renies, our history master. He goes about acting history scenes. He's acting now that this is the sea, that he's the king's son that was drowned in the sea and never smiled again."

"He must be *mad*," said the lady indignantly.

Mr Renies again made frenzied efforts to explain, but all he could do was to spit out lily buds.

"He's not exactly mad," said William indulgently, "He's just got this craze for actin' history scenes. I go about with him to see he doesn't do too much damage."

"But he's *ruining* the lily pond," said the lady.

"I know," said William sadly, "but he *would* go into it. When he thinks of a scene he wants to act nothin' can stop him."

The lady turned to Mr Renies indignantly.

"You ought to be ashamed of yourself," she said, "get out of my pond at once or I'll send for the police."

William had discreetly vanished into the dusk.

"Listen!" sputtered Mr Renies wildly, but the lady had turned on her heel and gone into the house, whither she sent a manservant to expel Mr Renies from the pond and to inform him that if he wasn't out of the garden within five minutes she was going to send for the police.

Dripping and dishevelled, Mr Renies stumbled out of the garden gate into the road. He peered about him, but there was no sign of William. Then from above his head came a small distinct voice.

"I'm actin' being Charles II in the oak tree now . . ."

Mr Renies ignored it. Wet, cold and hungry he staggered homewards.

Mr Renies' first thought was to lay the whole matter before the headmaster. For a boy to go to a master's house, eat his supper, ransack his drawers, hide in his cupboard, then lead him a dance over the countryside, was surely a crime unknown before in the annals of school life. Then Mr Renies began to wonder whether it would be really wise to lay the whole matter before the headmaster. The episodes that took place in his house were all right. It was the episodes that took place outside his house that made him hesitate. He saw himself clinging to those two girls, he saw himself floundering in the lily pond . . . Of course, he needn't mention those episodes, but he was beginning to know William a little better, and he was afraid that William's conscience would lead him to "confess" them. He saw himself the laughing-stock of the village. As things were, that might be avoided. He had heard one of the two girls say crossly: "That *awful* boy." Obviously they knew William and felt only annoyance with him. He could go to see the lady of the lily pond, and make up some story that would satisfy her. (He could say that he thought the boy had fallen into the lily pond and had plunged in to rescue him.) There wasn't any reason why anyone else should know anything about it. William might tell? Mr Renies had a shrewd idea that, properly treated, William would not tell . . .

He changed from his wet clothes and sat down to write to his cousin thanking him for the pheasant. He said with bitterness in his heart that it had been delicious. A funny thing about that boy, he reflected as he stamped and addressed the letter. He'd thought him a perfectly safe butt for his little jokes. One did sometimes make mistakes however . . .

The next morning Mr Renies entered the classroom, sat down at the master's desk, and said: "Open your note-books, please."

"Please, sir, aren't we going to have any acting today?" said a boy in the front row.

"Acting?" repeated Mr Renies, as if he did not understand.

"Yes, sir. Acting history scenes."

"Acting history scenes?" said Mr Renies in a tone of great surprise and indignation, "of course not. I never heard of such a thing. Open your note-books and take down the following dates." Then politely, almost affection-ately, in the tone in which a master speaks to a favourite pupil, he added: "Would you mind cleaning the board for me, please, Brown?"

A close observer would have noticed a rather peculiar smile on William's face, as he rose obediently from his desk and began to clean the board.

CHAPTER SEVEN

WILLIAM THE SUPERMAN

THE OUTLAWS, having met as usual at the corner of
William's road, ambled slowly along the road to
school engaged in desultory conversation.

William had propounded the question: "What would
you be if you couldn't be a yuman?" and the matter was
being discussed with animation. Ginger had chosen a lion,
Douglas an eagle, Henry a frog, and William a ghost, and
each was heatedly defending his choice. William's choice
had at first met with protest, but he had clung to it.

"*Course* a ghost's not a yuman. How could it be?
Can't eat, can it? All right, nex' time I see a ghost eatin'
I'll let you have it it's a yuman."

"You've never seen a ghost at all," objected Douglas.

"How d'you know I haven't?" said William, and
added with a sound that was meant to be a sarcastic laugh,
"I've *cert'nly* never seen one eatin'."

"Besides, it isn't eatin' that makes a yuman," said
Ginger, "animals eat."

"I never said it was, did I?" said William, "all I said
was you've never seen a ghost *eatin'*. Well, when you see
a ghost eatin' kin'ly come'n' tell me, that's all."

The air of triumph with which William said this made

143

the others feel somehow that they'd got the worst of the argument.

"Anyway," said William pursuing his advantage, "all you'll get killed or die of starvation same as what animals do, an' I'll go on livin' for ever, jumpin' out at people an' scarin' 'em stiff. I bet I have a better time than any of you. *Lions!*" he said contemptuously to Ginger, "they've nothin' to do all day but kill things an' eat 'em, an' I bet they have a rotten time gettin' bones an' horns' an' fur an' things in their throats. An'," his scorn deepened as he turned his gaze to Henry, "*frogs!*"

Henry felt that his choice needed defence, and began to defend it rather feebly.

"It's the splashin' I'd like," he said, "an' the hoppin' – great long hops."

"Hoppin'!" said Douglas scornfully. "What's hoppin' to shootin' through the air like what I'm goin' to do when I'm an eagle an' swooshin' down on things? Yes, an' I bet there won't be much left of *you* when you've been swooshed down on by me an' et in one mouthful."

"Yes an' I bet you'd be jolly soon as dead as me if you tried eatin' *me*. They don't eat frogs an' I bet it'd kill you."

"I bet they do."

"They don't."

"They do."

"They don't."

"An' you'd better look out for me when you're foolin' about catchin' frogs," said Ginger sternly to Douglas, "or I'll be springin' out at you an' that'll be the end of *you*."

"Oh *will* it," said Douglas with spirit. "Let *me* tell *you* that I'll be up again an' swooshin' down on *you* before you know where you are an' then there won't be much left of *you*."

William interrupted with a sinister laugh.

"Yes, an' you all wait till I get hauntin' the wood where you all are, an' there won't be much left of any of you. You'll be scared dead with me groanin' an' moanin' an' rattlin' chains an'—"

"Yes, you'll be groanin' an' moanin' all right when I—" began Ginger, then stopped.

They had reached the school door. A procession of boys wearing grey flannel suits was streaming into it, and in the procession appeared an amazing figure – dressed in a white sailor suit with long flapping trousers, and a white sailor's cap perched on a riot of golden curls. So jauntily and assuredly did it walk that the horror plainly visible on the faces around it was paralysed into silence. It passed on its way, leaving behind it a furious medley of sounds in which indignant small boys told each other all the things they were going to say to it the next time they saw it. The Outlaws forgot their imaginary rôles in the excitement.

"Who is he?"

"What's he comin' dressed up like that for?"

"Oughter be in a baby show, that's where *he* oughter be."

"I bet they turn him out."

But they didn't turn him out. When the Outlaws entered their form room, he was already seated at a desk, calmly examining some books and exercise books that had been given to him by the form master. Even the form master seemed slightly disconcerted by his appearance. He explained his presence shortly to the others. His father

145

had taken a house in the neighbourhood for a few months, and the headmaster had given him permission to attend the school while he was there. The headmaster unfortunately was not present to see the result of this permission. The headmaster was away with a nervous breakdown, and had left in charge the sixth form master – a muscular young man with a keen eye, upon whose notice William had always modestly shrunk from obtruding himself.

The form gazed with indignation at the white-clad curly-headed newcomer, restrained only from open demonstration by the presence of Authority. The white-clad child was wholly unmoved by their glances and comments. With an expression of the utmost complacency he settled himself down to receive – and impart – knowledge. His fluency was amazing, his French accent unexceptionable, his way with sums and problems breath-taking. The masters who visited them in the course of the morning commented on his ability, comparing it favourably with the ability of his classmates and drawing attention to his tender years (he was, as they were repeatedly informed during the morning, two years younger than any of them). Indignation against him rose higher each moment. But all attempts to express this indignation met with failure. Grimacing at him was like grimacing at a stone wall – a stone wall moreover with an impregnable conviction of its own superiority. A threat of stronger measures was met with: "All right. You *touch* me an' my father'll go to see your father an' *then* you'll catch it."

There was something so suggestive of anticipatory enjoyment on the part of the white-clad child, something so calm and assured as of a prophecy often fulfilled that the would-be assailant melted away. During the next

146

lesson, however, one of them managed to flick a large-sized ink blot on to the white sailor suit from his fountain pen when going up to write something on the board for the Latin master. On returning to his seat he sat down unsuspectingly into a little pool of ink. How it had come to be on his seat was a mystery. The white-clad child was apparently deeply absorbed in writing out the Latin for "The General, having summoned his soldiers, gave the signal for battle." But no one cared to experiment further upon the white suit. The Outlaws watched the newcomer with feelings of puzzled dislike, which grew stronger as the morning wore on. Their desks were too far removed from his to allow of their making personal experiment upon him, but they watched the experiments of their classmates with interest.

After school they followed him from the cloakroom to the road. The dapper, swaggering little figure had a strange fascination for them. It made its way to a large motor-car that stood in the road. A uniformed chauffeur leapt down to open the door for it. The Outlaws advanced nearer. Just as the white-clad child was about to step into the car, he turned and saw the Outlaws standing round him – an interested but hostile little group. His eyes met William's in a challenging stare.

"You'd look a bit better," said William sternly, "with your hair cut off."

"An' *you'd* looka bit better," said the amazing child without a moment's hesitation, "with your face cut off."

Then he stepped airily into the car and drove away, leaving the Outlaws gaping after him, open-eyed and open-mouthed.

"Well," said William shortly, "well, somethin' wants doin' to *him*."

It was evident that the others were entirely in agreement with this cryptic statement.

"What *he* wants," said Ginger vehemently, "is the *cheek* takin' out of him. An' I votes we start by cuttin' off his hair."

"Let's kidnap him," said William.

"In masks," put in Ginger eagerly.

"Take him to the old barn," said Henry.

"Cut his hair off an' dress him in proper clothes, and burn his ole white things."

"Wearin' masks all the time."

"Spring out at him from somewhere, an' tie him up an' carry him off to the ole barn."

"All wearin' masks."

The object of the kidnapping expedition was fading into insignificance before this sinister mental picture of four masked men leaping out of ambush . . .

"Let's hold up the car an' tie up the shofer . . ." said Ginger excitedly.

But despite their impressive vision of themselves, even Ginger felt this to be going a little too far and ended rather feebly, "I've seen it done on the pictures, anyway."

"No," said William firmly. "The shofer's not done nothin' to us. It's not fair to get him into trouble. No . . . it's this boy we've gotter kidnap. We've gotter knock some of the *cheek* out of him, that's what we've gotter do. We've gotter cut his hair off an' put some decent clothes on to him 'stead of those ole white things. I know where an ole suit of mine is what's put in the box-room ready for the rummage sale, an' I'll get it an' bring it to the ole barn an' I bet we'll knock some of the *cheek* out of him. We'll have a bonfire of his hair an' his ole white suit an' I bet he'll be scared stiff of us in masks an' things an' I bet *that'll* knock the *cheek* out of him."

Life had been rather dull lately, and the Outlaws welcomed the prospect of an adventure.

"We'll have to think it out very carefully," said William, "and we'll have to keep it jolly secret, too. We don't want Scotland Yard gettin' to hear of it."

The Outlaws agreed that they didn't want Scotland Yard getting to hear of it, and separated, having arranged to meet the next evening after school to arrange the details of the *coup*.

But before the next evening something had happened that took William's mind entirely off kidnapping. William was not on the whole susceptible. He did not easily fall a victim to feminine wiles. There had only been one serious love passage in his life, and that had been when he had lost his heart to Joan, the little girl next door, who had long since left the neighbourhood.

Though William had forgotten her, and now treated the whole race of girls with coldness and disdain, he would occasionally meet one whose likeness to Joan would stir a tender chord in his heart. And this was what happened this afternoon. She was about William's size and she had the demure, dimpled face and dark hair that always made him think of Joan. She met William in the road, looked at him with tentative friendliness, and said, "Hello!" It was the dimples (Joan had had them like that at the corners of her lips) that made him hesitate and finally return the greeting. He returned it scowling, in a fierce and threatening tone of voice, but he returned it, and then stood glaring at her waiting for her next move. Her next move was to dimple again and say: "What's your name?"

He scowled more fiercely than ever, muttered "William" and swung on his heel to walk away from her. She trotted lightly at his side. "Mine's Angela," she said. William unbent very slightly. "Is it?" he said.

"Yes," said the little girl, flattered by the interest implied in the question. "Yes, it is . . . William, do you go to school?"

"Course," said William gruffly.

"Do you go to the school here, William?"

"Yes."

She clasped her hands.

"Oh, William, *William*, will you do something for me?"

William looked at her. Blue eyes, fixed on him imploringly. Dimples still faintly visible.

"A'right," he said ungraciously. "What?"

"Look after my little brother, William. He's gone to that school too."

"A'right," said William. "A 'right, I'll look after him all right." His mind passed in a mental review the members of the junior forms, whom he treated usually with hauteur and contempt. It was going to be galling to his pride to display friendliness towards one of these inferior creatures, but – the dark eyes were fixed on him, the dimples coming and going anxiously, and William was as Samson shorn of his locks.

"A'right," he said again. "I'll look after him for you."

Her gratitude was touching.

"Oh, William!" she said, "I knew you would. I *knew* you were kind," – William hastily assumed an imbecile expression meant to imply kindness – "and I *know* he'll be all right if *you* look after him."

William uttered a short laugh – a laugh that hinted vaguely at a vast and sinister power.

"Oh, yes, I bet anyone's all right if *I* look after him. I bet anyone's *jolly well* all right if *I* look after him."

"You won't let anyone be unkind to him, will you, William?"

"No," said William, repeating his short laugh. "No. If anyone's unkind to him they'll be jolly sorry. I bet they won't do it twice. I bet, once they know *I'm* lookin' after him. I bet there's a lot of people what'll be scared of *lookin'* at him once they know *I'm* takin' care of him."

"Oh, *William!*"

Her eyes shone with an admiration that went to William's head like wine. His swagger became outrageous. He repeated his short laugh, which had now passed the fine point of perfection and become a rather meaningless snort.

"Then you *will* look after my little brother, William?" she repeated.

William was rather annoyed to have the little brother dragged into the conversation again. He didn't take any interest in the little brother. Again he passed the members of the junior form before his mental gaze. He hoped that it wasn't the one that squinted, or the one that howled when you looked at him. And he hoped that no one would see him speaking to the kid. And, above all, he hoped that she realised what she was asking of him.

"What's his name?" he said without enthusiasm.

"Reggie."

The name did little to inspire confidence. If it wasn't the one that squinted, it was sure to be the one that howled.

"What's he look like?" he said. "Does he squint?"

"Oh, *no*, William. He's *sweet*. He's a *darling*. He's got lovely curls and he always wears a white sailor suit."

The blood in William's veins turned to ice.

"What?" he said. "W-w-what?"

"He's sweet," repeated Reggie's sister, "and he's *ever* so clever, and you'll know him by his white sailor suit. Didn't you hear me say it the first time?"

William swallowed.

"No," he said faintly, "no, I din't quite hear the first time."

"Well, you'll be able to recognise him now, won't you?"

"Oh, yes," said William bitterly. "Yes, I'll be able to recognise him now all right."

"He goes to school in the car because his school's farther away than mine, and I'm older. You'll know him when you see him, William. He's *ever* so sweet."

"Oh, yes," said William again slowly, "I'll know him when I see him all right."

William made his way slowly and reluctantly to the meeting at the old barn.

Alas for the fickleness of man! With his faithful band of followers William had undergone innumerable adventures, risked innumerable perils, performed innumerable deeds of daring. And at a glance from a pair of dark eyes, at the flicker of a dimple in a pair of smooth cheeks, it was all to count for nothing. William was going to meet his comrades with treachery in his heart. They turned trusting eyes on him as he entered.

"Now," said Ginger, "now let's make up a plan. I've found out where he's livin'. The question is where's the best place to ambush him."

William assumed his best air of mystery.

"I've gotter plan," he said unblushingly, "I've gotter plan what's better'n that."

"What is it?" said Ginger.

"I've not got it quite ready yet," said William, "an' I'm not goin' to tell you till I've got it quite ready."

It is eloquent of the depths to which William had sunk that he met the trusting gaze of his followers without compunction.

"When'll you have it ready?" said Ginger.

"I don't know yet," said William, "an' we mustn't let him get suspicious. We mus' be all right to him so's he won't get suspicious of us. My plan won't be any good at all if he gets suspicious of us."

It was obvious that, though still trusting, his followers were disappointed.

"I don't see what was wrong with kidnappin' him in masks," said Ginger. "I think that was a jolly good plan."

"Well, wait till you hear mine," said the perfidious William.

"Well, what *is* yours?" challenged Ginger. "You tell us what yours is an' then p'raps we'll b'lieve it's better."

William put on his most irritatingly superior manner.

"All right," he said, "if you don't want my plan, you go on an' do your own. Go on an' kidnap him. I bet you'll be sorry when you find out what my plan is."

Even William was surprised (and, if the truth must be told, rather gratified than otherwise) at his skill in double-dealing. The assurance of his manner carried the day.

"A'right," said Ginger meekly. "A'right. Only I don't see why we can't know about it now. We might be doin' somethin' to help."

"You can," said William. "You can do somethin' to help. You can pretend to be nice to him. We've got to lure" (he meant lull) "his suspicions if my plan's goin' to come off all right."

All that evening as he moved about his home – doing his homework, sliding down the balusters, inadequately washing his hands, attending the family meals – William was conversing with the little girl. He was telling her of his heroic exploits . . . of how he had wrestled with a lion and killed it with his naked hands, how he had held at bay a hundred hostile Red Indians, armed with poisoned arrows, and how he had made his way alone and unarmed through the enemy's lines, bearded the hostile commander-in-chief in his tent, and forced him at the point of the sword to hand over all his maps and plans of battle. (William was vague as to the historical background of these exploits, but he had performed the exploits so often in imagination that the exploits themselves were more vivid than many things that had actually happened to him.)

In his mental recital of them to the little girl, he uttered his short scornful laugh so often that his father, who wasn't in a very good temper, said, "What on earth's the matter with you? If you want to clear your throat, clear it. Don't go choking about the place like that."

William gave him what he fondly imagined to be a crushing glance, and went out into the garden, where he told the little girl in imagination of how he had unmasked and handcuffed an international crook, whose appearance, as described by William, bore a striking resemblance to that of his father.

The next morning passed uneventfully. The white-clad child arrived in his limousine, superior and immaculate as ever. Despite the curls and white sailor suit, there was something about him that made his classmates give him a wide berth. They hadn't forgotten the little incident of the ink pool. All except the Outlaws. The Outlaws didn't give him a wide berth. They fussed about him in revolting friendliness, occasionally getting behind him to wink at William and double up in mirth, evidently deriving intense amusement from the thought of William's secret plan in which they were assisting.

William was at the corner of the road again when the little girl returned from school, and approached her with an appearance of truculence that would have effectively concealed his feelings from any observer, but that did not seem to alarm the little girl. She greeted him eagerly.

"Oh, *William*," she said, "how *nice* of you."

"I jus' happened to be here," said William with an elaborate unconcern that defeated its own ends. "I'd forgot that this was the time you came from school."

"Oh, *William*, I've been *longing* to see you again. Thank you so *much*. Reggie said that all the boys were so nice to him at school, and I'm *sure* it was because of you."

155

William laughed his short sinister laugh.

"Oh yes, it was because of me all right. I jus' told 'em they'd got to. There's not *many* people that'd dare do a thing I tell 'em not to. People that *know* me do as I tell 'em. They jolly well remember one or two things an'—" he hesitated a moment, wondering whether to introduce at this point the story of his wrestling with a lion and killing it with his naked hands, or the story of how he had held at bay a hundred hostile Red Indians, armed with poisoned arrows, or how he had made his way alone and unarmed through the enemy's lines. He'd worked them all up to such a fine pitch of perfection that he didn't want any of them to be wasted. She broke in, however, before he could introduce any of them.

"And he said that the masters were nice to him, too, but, of course, that's because he's so clever."

Again William laughed his short sinister laugh. It was so short and so sinister now that it startled a horse looking over the fence and it fled neighing to the other side of the field.

"Oh, no," said William. "I bet it wasn't that. No, it wasn't *that* all right."

His voice expressed amusement as at some dark secret.

"Oh, William, what was it then? It wasn't *you*, was it? You couldn't make the *masters* nice to him, surely?"

This seemed to amuse William intensely.

"Oh, couldn't I?" he said. "You don't *know* the things I c'n do . . ." And he managed to get in his story of how he had made his way alone and unarmed through the enemy's lines, bearded the hostile commander-in-chief in

156

his tent, and forced him at the point of the sword to hand over all his maps and plans of battle.

The little girl was impressed, but less impressed than by his alleged despotism over the staff of the school he attended.

"But, William, the *masters?* How do you make the *masters* do what you tell them to? You can't take a sword to school."

The mental picture thus evoked of his rising in his desk, and with drawn sword insisting on old Sparkie marking all his sums right was a pleasant one, but had to be abandoned as too difficult to substantiate.

He smiled a superior smile.

"Oh, no," he said, "I don't make 'em do what I want with a *sword*. Not a *sword* exactly. But I'll tell you what I did once. I was out walkin' in the jungle one day an' I suddenly heard an awful whizzin' noise, an' it was a lion leapin' down at me through the air from a tree where it'd crept to hide till I came along an' I jus' caught . . ."

But the little girl wasn't interested in the story of the lion. She believed it implicitly, but what she was interested in – passionately, morbidly interested in – was William's terrorising of the muscular young men who formed the staff of the local Grammar School.

"But, William, the *masters!* How do you make *them* do what you want them to?"

William was rather irritated at being dragged back from the free unhampered atmosphere of the jungle to the cramped atmosphere of the school room, with young men in grey flannel suits as antagonists instead of lions.

"Oh, I jus' do," he said vaguely, and then with a sudden inspired modesty, "I don' talk about it. It might

157

make other people jealous, so I don' tell people about it."

"Oh, but, *William*. William, do tell me. William, I won't tell *anyone* how you do it. William, I *promise* you I won't. Oh, *William*, I thought I was your friend." There was a hint of tears in her voice. William melted to it.

"I jus' *look* at 'em," he said darkly.

"Oh, but, William, you couldn't make them do things by just *looking*."

"Oh, cudn't I?"

William uttered his short laugh again. So short it had grown by now that the little girl threw him a glance of sympathy and said:

"Have you got hiccoughs, William? Isn't it a horrid feeling? Hold your breath an' count twenty."

"No," said William coldly, "I've not got hiccoughs, thanks."

"Well, do tell me what you do."

"I've told you. I *look* at 'em."

"But, William, *looking* at them *couldn't* make them *do* things."

"*My* lookin' at 'em does," said William with such emphasis that he convinced both himself and the little girl.

"Oh, William, show me. Show me how you look at them."

"I cudn't. I cudn't do it to you. It'd scare you so's you'd have nightmares every night all the rest of your life."

"Oh, William, do *they* have nightmares every night – the masters?"

William made as if to utter his short laugh again, then
thought better of it and smiled sardonically.

"I bet one or *two* of them do," he said.

"Oh, William, do show it me. Do do it."

He shook his head.

"No," he said. "I wun't do it to you. Ever. It's a norful
look."

"What sort of a look?" It was evident that the little
girl took a fearful pleasure in his strange power. "A *fierce*
sort of look?"

"Yes, it's so fierce that people that've once seen it
never forget it, an' what's more, they feel scared of me
all the rest of their lives."

He spoke with conviction. He was coming to believe
in his Look.

"But, William, you din't ever look at the *headmaster*
that way, did you? Not at Mr Ferris?"

She was thrilling with delicious terror at the thought.

"He's not the real head," said William with airy
contempt.

"But did you?" she persisted.

He laughed.

"Him? I should jus' think I did. I should jus' *think* I
did. He's jolly careful what he says to me now."

"Oh, *William! Tell* me about it."

"Oh, well. I jus' went to him . . ."

"To his house?"

"Yes, to his house. I jus' went to his house an' I
walked into the room where he was sittin' . . ."

"Oh, *William!*"

"I jus' walked in the room where he was sittin' an' I
stood an' looked at him."

"With your Look?"

"Yes. With my Look. I stood an' looked at him with my Look, an' I didn't say anythin' at first . . ."

William was warming to his theme. He could see the scene quite plainly.

"I jus' looked at him an' then I said: 'You'd jus' better look *out* what you do to me. That's what *you'd* better do'."

"An' what did he look like?"

"Same as people do on the pictures. His mouth open an' all scrunched up."

"Oh, I *know*. And then what happened?"

"What happened? I said: 'Jus' you jolly well don't forget *that!*'"

"And what did he say?"

"Him? Huh! Nothin'. He was too scared."

"An' after that did he leave you alone?"

"Huh! I should jolly well *think* so. He daren't speak to me or look at me now, he's so scared of me."

"Has he never spoke to you since?"

But William was growing tired of Mr Ferris. His Look was an idea worthy of larger scope, and already his fertile imagination was at work upon it. He was advancing stealthily upon a serried mass of Red Indians in war paint, fixing his eyes upon them with the terrible Look . . . they were dropping their poisoned arrows and turning to flee . . . He was advancing through the jungle, his head poked forward in a sinister fashion, the terrible Look upon his face. Lions, tigers, elephants, snakes, fled in a panic-stricken stampede before him . . .

"I'll tell you somethin' I once did—" he began, but the church clock struck, and with a "Oh, my goodness! I

160

shall be late for tea," she ran away down the road, turning at the corner to kiss her hand to him.

He stood for a moment, gazing at the spot where she had disappeared, a languishing smile on his face, but he was not allowed the enjoyment of these softer feelings for long.

Ginger, Henry and Douglas appeared at the spot where he was gazing languishingly, and his expression changed abruptly to his customary scowl.

"*Now* tell us about that plan," they shouted as they leapt down the road to him.

The plan – he'd forgotten the plan. He gazed at them distatefully. After the little girl they looked singularly unattractive.

"What plan?" he said.

They stared at him blankly.

"*What* plan?" they repeated. "The plan for takin' the cheek out of him an' cuttin' off his curls, of course."

"Oh, *that*," said William loftily. "Well, I bet I've had other things to think of than that."

"You've – *what?*" they said indignantly. "But you said you'd gotter *plan*. You told us that the beginnin' of it was to lure his suspicions, an' you'd tell us the rest when we'd done that. Well, haven't we been doin' that all mornin'? Haven't we been lurin' his suspicions, 'stead of cuttin' his hair off at once same as we wanted to, jus' 'cause of your ole plan. Well, what *is* it, that's what we want to know?"

They were staring at him mutinously. He turned on them with a ferocious grimace that was meant to represent his Look. The result was disappointing. They retorted by grimaces fiercer and more effective.

"You'd jolly well like to know what it is, wouldn't

you?" he said mockingly. "Oh, yes, I bet you'd jolly well like to know."

"Yes, an' if you don't tell us," said Ginger threateningly, "we'll stop helpin' you."

"I picked up his pencil for him today," said Douglas morosely.

"An' I said good mornin' to him," said Henry, and repeated with fierce indignation, "Good *mornin'*. To *him*."

"An' we're *sick* of your ole plan that never comes off," said Ginger, "an' if you won't tell us we'll have one on our own an' kidnap him."

"Oh, will you!" jeered William, "I'd jolly well like to see you."

He felt, however, more uncomfortable than he sounded.

Though he'd never heard the phrase "between the devil and the deep sea," he quite appreciated its meaning.

"Yes an' we'll kidnap you, too, if you aren't careful," said Ginger.

"Oh, will you! You'll have to catch me first. Come on . . . catch me . . . Come on!"

In the exciting chase that followed all four Outlaws forgot how it had begun.

William woke up the next morning with a distinct feeling of uneasiness that was partly retrospective and partly anticipatory. Certainly the thought of the little girl and her admiration still thrilled him, but, the more he thought over what he had said to her yesterday, the more uneasy he felt. He'd definitely told her that he could assume a look that struck terror to the heart of even that redoubtable athlete Mr Ferris. Her belief in him was

162

touching and inspiring, but any chance might discredit his story and he could not bear the thought of losing her admiration. Moreover, there were the Outlaws clamouring for his "plan", becoming more mutinous and turbulent every minute. How could he stop them laying violent hands upon the sacred form of Reggie, and how could he face her if they did?

Fortunately the early morning left no time to ponder on the problem, and William, flying breathlessly from his bed to breakfast and from breakfast to school – always five minutes late – was at his desk in his form room before he had time to consider the situation again.

And here the situation forced itself upon his notice in the very first period.

The mathematical master (known as Sparkie) was away with influenza, and Mr Ferris took them for arithmetic in his place. Without exactly seeing where the danger lay, William was vaguely aware that the situation was fraught with danger. He decided that the best way of meeting it was to obliterate himself from public notice as far as possible. He applied himself earnestly to the first sum put up on the board by Mr Ferris, which had to do with the time taken by two men to cut down eighty-eight trees at the rate of one every two hours.

"Give you an easy one to start with," he had said with that misplaced brightness that schoolmasters bring to bear on such subjects.

William had moved his desk slightly so that Henry's back hid him from the gaze of Authority. He sat working in an almost painful silence and immobility hardly daring to breathe lest he should bring upon himself that vague catastrophe that he felt sure the situation contained.

But he knew, of course, that Fate was not so easy to evade as that, and it was with a sinking of the heart but without surprise that he heard Mr Ferris say:

"You, Brown, read out your answer."

"Forty pounds, four shillings, sir," read William in a tone of deprecating politeness.

There was a silence broken by Reggie's laugh.

It was not a laugh of honest amusement. It was a superior snigger. The acting head turned upon him.

"What's the matter with *you?*" he demanded curtly.

"Nothing sir," said Reggie.

"What are you laughing at then?"

"That boy's answer," said Reggie.

"All right. You can stay in an hour after school and do a few more sums as they amuse you so much."

"I'm having a music lesson after school today," objected Reggie.

"You can stay in an hour and a half tomorrow then instead."

This sentence was greeted with subdued triumph by the form. William's delight alone was tempered by apprehension. He was very thoughtful for the rest of the day, and set off homewards promptly after afternoon school in order to avoid the meeting with the little girl. The little girl, however, was there at the corner waiting for him. He saw at once that she was distressed. She greeted him without the dimples.

"Oh, William! He says he's got to stay in tomorrow. William, he's *never* been kept in before all his life. Oh, William, *do* make him say he needn't."

"Me?" said William faintly.

"Yes . . . Oh, William, he didn't do *anything*. They

164

had a sum about how many days it would take some woodcutters to cut down some trees, and some *stupid* boy said pounds instead of days and Reggie laughed. Well, William, wouldn't *you* have laughed if some stupid boy had said pounds instead of days?"

"Me?" said William again feebly.

"Yes. Oh, William, I can't bear him to be kept in. He's never been kept in before. William, do make him let him off."

"Me?" said William yet again.

"Yes... you know... You can. You *know* you can go to him an' look at him with your Look an' tell him to an' he'll have to. You *know* you can, William."

"Yes," said William desperately, "I know I can, an' I wish I'd got time to but I simply haven't got time to. I'm late for tea now an' then I've got my homework an' that'll take me till bedtime so that I simply haven't got time to. An' I'm busy every *minute* tomorrow. I'm sorry an' I would if I'd got time to, but I simply haven't."

They had been walking slowly down the road, and had now reached the small Georgian house where Mr Ferris lived. William observed this with secret horror, and tried to hasten past it, but the little girl had halted at the gate.

"Oh, William, it won't take you a minute. This is his house an' you can go in *now* an' ask him. William, do. William, *please* do. William, I thought you *liked* me."

"I do," said the goaded William. "I tell you I *do* like you. I-I-I-don't want to go scarin' him now he's got ole Markie's work to do's well as his own. If I went scarin' him mos' prob'ly he'd have to go away for a rest cure same as old Markie, an' then there'd be no one to look after the school an' *I'd* get into trouble. Well, they might put me in prison for it an – an'," he decided that the colours might as well be laid on thick, "an' I might die of hunger and rats crawling over me same as people in pictures."

But this harrowing description left her unmoved.

"Oh, you couldn't, William, you *couldn't*. You need't look at him *much*. Jus' enough to make him say that Reggie needn't stay in. You needn't frighten him dreadfully. Just do your Look. You know William. The way you do. Oh, William, do *do*, DO! William, if you don't it means that you don't love me a bit! Oh, *William!*"

William gazed into her tear-filled eyes and was lost.

"A'right," he muttered, "a'right, I'll go."

"Oh, William. I *knew* you would."

William made great play of straightening his collar and tie and pulling up his stockings. After all every second helped. Anything might happen to relieve the situation. Mr Ferris might fall dead suddenly of heart disease, as people did in books. There continued to be no signs in the house of this sudden calamity, however, and when his tie had been straightened so that it was impossible to straighten it any more, and his stockings pulled up till it was impossible to pull them up any more, there was nothing to do but to walk slowly and draggingly up to the front door. His heart was a leaden weight in the pit of his stomach. His one comfort was that the little girl could not hear what was said at the front door.

He raised the knocker and let it fall. A housemaid appeared at the door.

William moistened his dry lips and spoke in a hoarse voice.

"'Scuse me," he said, "but can you please tell me if Mr Jones lives here?"

The housemaid stared at him indignantly. She saw him pass the house every morning on his way to school, and she knew that he knew quite well that Mr Ferris lived there.

"'*Course* he don't," she said, and added threateningly, "and get off with you!"

William got off with him as quickly as possible, assuming, however, an arrogant swagger and stern expression as he reached the road.

"I'm sorry," he said regretfully, "she says he's out now an' so I'm afraid I can't do it. An' I've got to be gettin' home quick now or I'll be late for tea an'—"

"But, William, he *isn't* out. I've *seen* him through the window. She was telling a story. William, *do* go again. Go an' say that you *know* he's there. Go an' *make* him say Reggie needn't be kept in. Oh William, *please*."

Again her eyes brimmed with beseeching tears. William turned and walked very very slowly up to the front door again. He had propped the gate open in case his retreat should be a precipitous one. He raised the knocker and dropped it. The housemaid reappeared.

"'Scuse me," said William in a lifeless tone, his eyes fixed stonily upon her waistband, "'scuse me but I've forgotten if you said that Mr Jones lived here or not."

And then, just as the housemaid was opening her mouth to reply in obvious indignation, the tall and muscular figure of Mr Ferris appeared in the passage.

"What is it?" he said sharply. "What do you want? Come in here."

Nightmare horror closed upon William as he entered

the acting headmaster's study. He swallowed hard and fixed his blank gaze upon the ceiling.

"Well," said the acting headmaster again, "what is it?"

William tried to speak but his throat was dry. Then quite suddenly inspiration and his voice came to him at the same moment.

"P-please, sir," he said, "I-I din't quite understand one part of the lesson you gave us this mornin'."

The acting headmaster threw a sharp glance of suspicion at the boy who made this astounding statement, but, though pale, the boy looked earnest enough. It was obviously no practical joke.

"Well," he said. "What part was it?"

His tone was not encouraging. It was the first visit of this sort he had received and he meant it to be the last.

As William's memory of the arithmetic lesson was a complete blank, it was as well that Mr Ferris took down the book, opened it, and handed it to him.

"It was this," said William putting his finger down at random on the page.

"It's quite simple," said the acting headmaster curtly, "you can't have been listening."

He gave a short sharp explanation and ended:

"That's quite clear, isn't it? Good afternoon."

William swaggered down the path to the little girl.

"Oh, *William*!" she said clasping her hands. "Is it all right? Has he promised?"

William uttered his short sinister laugh.

"I bet I've scared him," he said. "I bet he'll think twice before he keeps your brother in again."

"But William, did he say he needn't stay in tomorrow? Did he *promise*?"

"He din't *axchully* promise," admitted William, "but" – he assumed his swagger again – "but I bet I *scared* him all right. Huh! I bet I *scared* him. I bet everyone'll find him a bit different after *this*."

"Oh but, William, *do* make him promise. Oh, William, I shan't sleep a minute tonight unless he axchully promises. Oh *William*!"

And such power had the beseeching eyes that before William knew what he was doing he found himself again on Mr Ferris' door-step raising the knocker. The house-maid, who appeared almost immediately, gazed at him open-mouthed, her indignation fading into a sort of fascinated horror at this, his third appearance.

Without taking her eyes from him, she called faintly over her shoulder.

"It's that boy again, sir."

And from the study came an irritated "What the dickens does he want *now*? Come in here, whats-your-name!"

William entered.

"Well, what d'you want *now*?" said Mr Ferris sharply.

William swallowed several times, and finally said in a hoarse and indistinct voice:

"Please, sir, I thought you beckoned to me from the window."

"You thought I b—? *Get* out and if I see any more of you—"

But William was already hastening down the garden path.

"'S all right," he said in rather a shaken voice to the little girl, "he's *axchully* promised now."

"Oh, *William*!" Her gratitude and relief were comforting. "Oh, William, you *are* clever. I'm *so* grateful. I'll go'n' tell Reggie now. He's been *terribly* upset. An' I'm goin' to buy a little present for him 'cause he's been so *terribly* upset. I've got sixpence. William, do come an' help me choose something for him."

William, shaken as he was by the ordeal through which he had just passed, nevertheless showed a touching interest in Reggie's present. For William had vivid memories of a certain cake, consisting chiefly of butter cream, obtainable at the village confectioner's, that had once incapacitated him for two days. On that occasion William had eaten twelve of them at a sitting. He had, after that occasion, so completely lost the taste for them it was difficult to realise now that they had once been nectar and ambrosia to him, but still the fact remained that they had been, and there was no reason why they shouldn't be to Reggie, nor was there any reason why they shouldn't have the same effect on him as they had had on William. It was a pleasant and consoling thought . . . Reggie undergoing the agonies that had convinced William that he was on his deathbed . . . Reggie returning to school a few days later, a pale and chastened shadow of his former self. The detention would be forgotten, of course, and William would still occupy his cherished and hard-won position of hero in the little girl's heart.

"Those are the ones," he said persuasively to the little girl, as they stood with their faces glued to the window. "Those there. I bet he'd sooner have some of those for a present than *anything*."

"Oh, but *William!*" she said aghast, "they look *awful*."

"They're not," he assured her. "They're *rippin'*!"

"They don't look as if they were a bit good for you."

"Oh, but they are," said William unblushingly. "They're jolly good for you. If ever I'm feelin' weak, I buy some of those an' they make me feel strong again d'rectly."

"How many shall I get?"

"Get twelve. They're a halfpenny each. Spend all your sixpence on them."

"Oh *William!*"

"Go on. He'll be jolly grateful, I bet. They'll cheer him up like anything. I *bet* they will."

He drew her, half reluctant, into the shop and said firmly:

"Sixpennoth of cream blodges, please. Big 'uns."

When, leaving the little girl at her gate, he finally departed homewards, he felt more hopeful than an hour ago he would have believed possible.

The next day he got up early, and made his way to the house where Reggie and the little girl lived. He hoped to see a doctor's car at the door, but the drive was empty. He looked up at the windows hoping to see a white-clad nurse, or at any rate some signs of desperate illness, but all he saw was Reggie, leaning out of the window, becurled and white-suited as usual and looking riotously healthy. Dismay closed over him once more.

He was turning to walk thoughtfully homeward, when he heard a shout behind him, and turned to see the little girl running after him down the road.

"Oh, *William*!" she called. "William, I was jus' comin' to your house to *tell* you. William, we're going away. William, I *hate* leaving you, but isn't it exciting?"

"Goin' away?" said William blankly.

"Yes. My daddy's got to go to America on business, an' he's got to be there for a year an' we're all goin' with him. And he's got to go at *once* and we're all going tomorrow. And we're not going to school today because we're going to help pack and – oh, William, if it wasn't for leaving *you* I'd be so excited. William, *do* say you'll miss me."

"Yes, I'll miss you," said William.

But his dismay at her news was tempered by relief. It simplified a situation that was growing too complicated even for William. After all, better lose the little girl and keep her admiration, than keep the little girl and lose her admiration.

"Reggie's sorry to leave school," she said, "because he's so fond of his lessons."

William turned from a mental picture of himself as seen by the little girl to a mental picture of Reggie and the cream blodges.

"Did – did he eat them?" he said wonderingly.

"Yes," said the little girl. "He ate them just before supper. He *loved* them."

"Jus' – jus' before supper?" said William feebly. "Did – did he eat his supper after them?"

"Oh *yes*. It was his favourite supper, you see. It was trifle with lots of cream."

Despite his curls and white suit and unbounded cheek, there was something about Reggie that inspired unwilling respect. Twelve cream blodges and then trifle with lots of cream. The thought brought a strange unpleasant qualm even to that hard-boiled organ, William's stomach.

"Well," he said, "I'd better be gettin' back home to breakfast."

"William, will you meet me tonight after school to say good-bye *properly*?"

"A'right," said William graciously.

Reggie's absence created a certain amount of interest, which William made the most of.

"Where is he?" he said with a sinister laugh in answer to Ginger's question. "Yes, I bet there's a lot of people would like to know that. I bet a lot of people would like to know where he is. You said I'd not gotter plan, din't you? Well p'raps you'll think a bit different now. Huh! Yes, I bet a lot of people would like to know where he is."

This attitude was rather effective till the form master, over-officiously as William thought, explained Reggie's disappearance. Even that, however, William carried off rather well.

"Oh yes," he said darkly, "his father's got to go to America. Oh yes. Oh yes, an, *why's* his father got to go to America?"

"On business," explained Henry simply.

William laughed. "Huh! Oh yes, that's what he *says*. That's what he *says* all right. Yes, that what he *says*. Yes, I din't let you into my plan 'cause it was a bit too dangerous. Yes, it's a bit dangerous, let me tell you, gettin' a whole family drove out of a country like this. Yes, I bet you'd be s'prised if I told you some of the adventures I've had over this, but I'd said I'd get 'em drove out of the country an' I have. It takes more 'n a few spies an' villains an' such-like to scare *me*."

But even William couldn't carry it off, and, as the morning wore on and their incredulity increased, he found it necessary to resort to physical violence on the person of anyone who mentioned his "plan".

He still felt light-hearted with relief at Fate's intervention, however, when he went to his farewell interview with the little girl. He was rather looking forward to that last interview with her. There were some finishing touches to be put to the portrait of him that he hoped to leave in her mind.

She was waiting for him at the spot where they generally met.

"Oh, William," she greeted him. "It's *dreadful* saying good-bye to you. William, I've written a note saying good-bye *properly*" – she gave him a note which he slipped complacently into his pocket – "for you to read when I've gone. Oh, William, I shall think of you every single day. I do *love* you, William."

"It's quite all right," said William in a tone of vague politeness.

"William, Mr Ferris came to see us this afternoon, and I thanked him for letting Reggie off staying in, though, of course, he couldn't help doing what you told him to."

The smile froze on William's face. "You – you said that?" he said faintly.

"Yes," said the little girl innocently, "and we talked about you an' how you can make people do what you want them to do by jus' lookin' at 'em. An' I said, didn't he feel *awful* the first time you went to him – the time you scared him almost to death, you know, an' said, 'You jus' better look *out* what you do to *me* an' jus' you jolly well don't forget *that*'."

A strange icy sensation was playing up and down William's spine.

"You – you said that?" he said in a whisper that was only just audible.

"Yes," said the little girl.

"An' – an' what did he say?" whispered William.

The solid earth seemed to have been cut away from under his feet. He was suspended in mid-air.

"He said, yes, he felt *awful*. I tried to make him 'scribe to me what you looked like, when you had your Look on, 'cause I told him you wouldn't do it to me 'cause of scarin' me, an' he said it was too *terrible* to 'scribe."

William's eyes were protruding with horror, but with an almost superhuman effort he retained his fixed and ghastly smile.

"Yes," he said. "Well, I'd better be gettin' on or I'll be late for tea."

He took his leave of her as in a dream, and walked homewards as in a nightmare. The only possible solution of the situation, he decided, was for the end of the world to come now at once, but William had learnt by experience that that event never takes place when summoned.

"No," he said to himself bitterly. "No, if it comes at all, it'll prob'ly come when I've jus' caught a fish an' before I've had time to show it to anyone, or when someone's jus' brought me an ice cream an' before I've had time to eat it," and added, addressing the event with a fierce sardonic bitterness, "yes, that's what you jus' *would* do."

He entered the house gloomily.

His mother was in the kitchen, taking advantage of the cook's afternoon out to make a cake. He stood at the door, watching her morosely. It says much for the blackness of his spirit, that he made no attempt to secure any of the uncooked cake mixture for which he had a passion.

"Aren't you rather late home, dear?" said his mother. "Mr Ferris has just come to see your father. They're in the morning-room."

William thought that he had that afternoon plumbed the depth of horror, but he found that further depths remained, for, at this statement, it was as if his stomach had been suddenly wafted away from him, leaving a vacuum in its place.

"What's he come for?" he said at last, hoarsely.

"I don't know," said Mrs Brown. "He just asked to speak to your father, and I took him in there. I do hope you haven't been getting into any mischief, William."

Even in this ruin of William's fortune, his face mechanically assumed its look of outraged innocence.

"Me?" he said in the tone of offended surprise that, like his look of innocence, seemed to come of its own accord to meet a familiar need. "No. 'Course not."

He went draggingly out into the garden.

In the garden he remembered suddenly that Mr Luton of Jasmine Villas had slipped on a banana skin in the village street and broken his leg. It was an idea . . . They couldn't do anything to you if you'd got a broken leg.

He crept into the dining-room, took a banana from a dish on the sideboard, ate it, and carried the skin out to the garden. There he carefully laid it on a path, returned to the end of the path, then advanced jauntily, head in air. He walked over it ten times, without success. He couldn't even slip on the thing, much less break his leg on it. Next he climbed to the roof of the summer-house and fell from it, meaning to break his collar-bone. (They couldn't do anything to you if you'd got a broken collar-bone.) He landed unhurt on his feet. At this point he heard his mother calling from the front door.

"William, your father wants you."

William shot into the tool-shed like an arrow from a bow, and crouched behind the wheelbarrow.

"William!"

He didn't stir. There was silence except for the sound of his heart beating. It was beating so loud that he was afraid it would betray his hiding-place if his mother came out to look for him . . .

"William!"

That was his father. William recognised the tone of voice. He rose and dragged himself reluctantly into the morning-room. His father stood by the fireplace, and Mr Ferris sat in an arm-chair. There was a very peculiar expression on Mr Ferris' face.

William fixed his eyes on the ceiling. His brow was wet with perspiration. His throat was dry. His knees were unsteady.

"William," said his father, "Mr Ferris tells me that you went round to his house the other evening to ask him to explain something in the Arithmetic lesson that you hadn't quite understood. He says that he's glad to see you take such an interest in your work, and he's kindly offered to give you an hour's extra Arithmetic after school every day for the next fortnight."

Mr Brown's voice showed his bewilderment. It was clear that that was all Mr Ferris had told him, and that

Mr Brown was mystified. He kept trying to imagine William going round to Mr Ferris' house to ask him to explain something in the Arithmetic class that he hadn't understood, and he couldn't. He could swallow a lot of things but he strained at that. Still – if Mr Ferris said that it had happened, it must have happened. Perhaps they

WILLIAM FIXED HIS EYES ON THE CEILING. HIS THROAT WAS DRY, HIS KNEES WERE UNSTEADY.

had all misjudged poor William – even the masters who gave him such execrable reports term after term. Perhaps William really took an interest in his work after all . . .

"WILLIAM," SAID HIS FATHER, "MR FERRIS TELLS ME THAT YOU WENT ROUND TO HIS HOUSE THE OTHER EVENING."

"Well, aren't you going to say thank you?" he said sharply to his son.

"Thank you, sir," said William to the ceiling.

He simply couldn't meet that peculiar expression in Mr Ferris' eye.

In the garden he climbed on to the fence to consider the situation. An hour every day for a fortnight. The only hour that was ever left when he'd finished his homework. No games with his Outlaws, except at the week-end, for a fortnight. He plunged his hands into his pocket in search of consolation, and found some string, a penknife, a piece of putty, and the little girl's note. He opened it and read:

Dere William,

I think that you are the most wunderful pursun in the wurld. I shal nevver forget you.

His frown lightened despite himself.

In the little girl's imagination at any rate that sinister omnipotent figure of William's dreams would live on . . .

"William!"

It was his mother. She carried a bowl in her hands.

"William, I thought you might like to scrape this out."

She had left a shamelessly large portion of her mixture in it, half a cake at least.

(Mrs Brown had been most indignant at her husband's incredulity.

"Of *course* he went to Mr Ferris because he wanted to understand his Arithmetic. Why should Mr Ferris say he did, if he didn't? I think it's most *unfair* to William

180

not to believe it. I've always *thought* that William must be better at his work than they make out. I've *never* believed those awful reports he gets.")

"Here you are, dear. The spoon's in it. And, William, I'm so glad that you're beginning to take such an interest in your work. I'm very much pleased about it."

"Uh-huh!" said William modestly. She returned indoors. He scrambled down from the fence, and went to the wheelbarrow that had been left under the tree at the end of the lawn. Lying in it full length, he began slowly and with lingering relish to eat the delicious mixture. Jumble came running across the lawn, leapt upon him and sat down firmly upon his stomach. Jumble, too, loved "raw cake," and William divided it with him, giving them a spoonful each in turn.

Lying there in the wheelbarrow in the perfect summer evening with Jumble sitting on his stomach and this bowl of the food of the Gods in his arms, it was difficult to feel despondent, even with the prospect of that fortnight's bondage staring him in the face. After all, a fortnight has to come to an end sometime. It can't last for ever . . .

As he scraped out the last spoonful and put it into his mouth, he thought of that peculiar expression on Mr Ferris' face – eyes twinkling, lips compressed to keep them steady – and it suddenly occurred to him that even that fortnight might not be so bad.

CHAPTER EIGHT

THE OUTLAWS' REPORT

WILLIAM PLODDED ALONG the road, his school satchel over his shoulder, his hands in his pockets. He was collecting keys for metal salvage, and so far he had met with fairly good results. Large keys, little keys, rusty keys, bright keys, door keys, cupboard keys, attaché-case keys, jewel-case keys, ignition keys, jingled behind him as he walked . . . But he wasn't thinking of keys. He was thinking of the conversations he had overheard at the houses where he had called. They had nearly all been on the same topic . . . "Reconstruction" . . . "better conditions" . . . "shorter hours" . . . "higher wages" . . . "freedom from want and fear" . . . "the Beveridge Report" . . . His brow was deeply furrowed as he plodded along to the old barn, where he had arranged to meet the other Outlaws and compare results in key collecting.

Ginger, Douglas and Henry were already there when he arrived, engaged in counting their spoils.

"We've got over a hundred altogether so far," said Ginger excitedly. "How many have you got, William?"

William dumped his satchel down in a corner, still frowning abstractedly.

"Dunno," he said. "Look here! Everyone's talkin'

about better conditions an' shorter hours an' things, an' what I want to know is what's goin' to happen to *us*?"

"What about?" said Henry.

"Well, everyone else is goin' to get a jolly good time after the war, but no one's thinkin' of *us*. Jus' 'cause we've not got a vote or anythin' we're not goin' to come in for any of it. What about shorter hours an' more money an' all the rest of it for *us*? I bet we could do with a bit of freedom from want an' fear, same as anyone else."

"Yes, I bet we could," agreed the others.

"I don't see why grown-ups should get everything an' us nothin'."

"How do grown-ups get it?" asked Douglas.

"They've got a thing called a Beveridge Report," explained William.

"Why can't we have one?"

"This Beveridge man's grown-up," said William bitterly. "So he only cares about grown-ups. We've gotter do somethin' for ourselves if we want anythin' done at all."

"The Outlaws' Report," suggested Henry.

"Yes, that's it. The Outlaws' Report ... An' we'd better get it goin' pretty quick ... Let's go to your house, Ginger. It's the nearest."

In Ginger's bedroom they squatted down on the floor to compose the terms of the Outlaws' Report, and Ginger tore the two middle pages from his Latin exercise-book and handed them to William.

"That'll do to write it down on," he said. "We've gotter have it same as theirs ..."

"Well, first of all, they're goin' to have shorter hours," said William. "So we'll have 'em too."

"Longer holidays," said Ginger.

"*Much* longer holidays," said Henry.

"As much holidays as term," said Douglas.

"*More* holidays than term," said Ginger.

"We'd better not ask for *too* much," said William, "or we may not get it. We'll ask for as much holidays as term. That's only fair. Well, it stands to reason that, when we've wore out our brains for – say, three months, we oughter have three months for our brains to grow back to their right size again. Well, you've only gotter think of trees an' things," vaguely. "They've got all winter to rest in. Their leaves come off at the end of summer an' don't come on again till the nex' summer, an' I bet our brains oughter be as important as a lot of ole leaves."

The Outlaws, deeply impressed by the logic of this argument, assented vociferously.

"Hollidays as long as term," wrote William slowly and laboriously.

"An' no afternoon school," suggested Ginger.

"Yes, no afternoon school," agreed William. "Afternoon school's not nat'ral. Well, come to that, school's not nat'ral at all. Look at animals. They don't go to school an' they get on all right. Still, I don't s'pose they'd let us give up school altogether, 'cause of schoolmasters havin' to have somethin' to do. Axshally, I don't see why schoolmasters shouldn't teach each other. It'd give 'em somethin' to do *an'* serve 'em right. Still, we'll be reas'nable. We'll jus' put down 'Holidays as long as term an' no afternoon school' . . . Then there's 'Higher Wages'."

"Yes," said Ginger, "that's jolly important. I could do with a bit of higher wages, all right."

"Let's say, 'Sixpence a week pocket money'," suggested Henry.

"An' not to be took off for anythin'," said Ginger. "They're always takin' mine off me for nothin' at all. Jus' meanness. I bet they've made *pounds* out of me, takin' my pocket money off for nothin' at all."

"Yes, we'll put that in," said William, and wrote: "'Sixpence a week pocket munny, and not to be took off.' Now what comes next? What other Better Conditions do we want?"

"No Latin," said Ginger firmly.

"No French," said Douglas.

"No Arithmetic," said Henry.

"No, none of *them*," agreed William firmly, adding this fresh demand to the list. "I bet we can get on without *them*, all right."

"What about no hist'ry?" suggested Ginger.

"Well, we've gotter keep *somethin'* for schoolmasters to teach," said William indulgently. "Hist'ry isn't bad, an' English isn't bad, 'cause ole Sarky can't see what you're doin' at the back, an' Stinks isn't bad, 'cause you can get some jolly good bangs if you mix the wrong things together. We'll jus' keep it at, 'No Latin or French or Arithmetic'."

"What else is there?" said Henry.

"Well, they're very particular about 'Freedom from Want an' Fear'," said William. "We've gotter be particular about that, too."

"That means no punishments," said Douglas.

"Yes, that's only fair," said William. "*They* can break things an' be late for meals an' get cross and forget things an' answer each other back an' do what they like an' nothin' ever happens to *them*, so I don't see why it should to us. It's about time *we* had a bit of this equality what people are always talkin' about."

"Well, let's put that down," said Ginger. "No punishments and stay up as late as we like."

"An' what about food?" said Douglas. "We'd better put down somethin' about that. We need somethin' more than sixpence a week to give us freedom from want. I bet I wouldn't feel free from want – not *really*, not *honestly* free from want – without six ice creams a day."

"*An'* bananas – after the war."

"*An'* cream buns." ·

"Yes, *an'* cream buns."

"An' bull's-eyes. Lots an' lots of them. As many as we want."

"An' we can't buy all that out of sixpence a week, so it ought to be extra."

"Yes, it jolly well oughter be extra."

They contemplated this blissful prospect in silence for some moments, then William said, "Now let's get it all put down prop'ly. Give us another piece of paper, Ginger."

Ginger tore several more sheets from the middle of his mutilated Latin exercise-book.

"It won't matter," he said carelessly, "'cause we won't be doin' Latin any more after we get this Report thing fixed up."

William took a sheet and wrote: "Outlaws' Report" at the head of it.

"They're goin' to make this Beveridge Report thing into an Act of Parliament," he said, "so we oughter do somethin' about gettin' ours made into one."

"What can we put that means that?" asked Ginger.

They all looked at Henry, who was generally considered the best informed of the Outlaws.

"I think it's Habeas Corpus," said Henry. "That's somethin' to do with it anyway."

"No, it isn't. It's Magna Charta," said Douglas. "I'm *sure* it's Magna Charta."

"We'll put both in," said William pacifically, "so as to be on the safe side. How do you spell 'em?"

"Dunno," said Douglas, and Henry, who never liked to own himself at a loss, said airily: "Oh, jus' as they're pronounced."

Carefully, laboriously, William wrote:

Outlaws Report.
Habby. Ass. Corpuss.
Magner Carter.

1. As much hollidays as term.
2. No afternoon school.
3. Sixpence a week pocket munny and not to be took off.
4. No Latin no French no Arithmetick.
5. As much ice creem and banarnas and creem buns as we like free.
6. No punnishments and stay up as late as we like.

He looked up from his labours, frowning intently.

"Is there anythin' else?" he said.

The Outlaws drew deep breaths of ecstasy.

"No," said Ginger in a trance-like voice, "if we get that, it'll be all right. We'll be freed from want an' fear then, all right."

"Well, what do we do about it now?" said William.

They awoke slowly and reluctantly from dreams of unlimited ice cream, bananas and holidays . . .

"We've gotter get it made into an Act of Parliament," said Ginger. "How do we start?"

"Well," said Henry rather uncertainly, "I suppose we've got to write to the Government about it."

"That wouldn't be any good," said William. "It never is. D'you remember when we wrote to the Government asking them to let us be commandos, an' they never even answered? An' the time we wrote to them, askin' them to shut all the schools an' send all the schoolmasters out to the war to finish it off quick, 'cause of them all bein' so savage, an' they never even answered that."

"We ought to take it to Parliament ourselves."

"They wouldn't let us in."

"Then we ought to give it to a Member of Parliament to take."

"That wouldn't be any good. There's only one Member of Parliament round here, and he's been mad at us ever since we tried to turn his collie into a French poodle."

"Then we've gotter find someone else high-up what's goin' to London to see the Government and will take it for us."

"I *know!*" said Ginger with a sudden shout. "There's Major Hamilton. He's high-up in the War Office, an' he's been home for the week-end, an' he's going back this mornin'. Let's ask him to take it."

The Outlaws' faces glowed with eagerness, then gradually the glow faded.

"That wouldn't be any good," said Douglas with a pessimism born of experience. "People don't take any

"WE GOTTER GET IT MADE INTO AN ACT OF PARLIAMENT," SAID
WILLIAM.

notice of children. It's jus' 'cause this ole Beveridge man's grown-up, that they make all this fuss of him. Ours is jus' as good, but I bet they won't take any notice of it."

"Let's go an' see, anyway," said William. "Where does he live?"

"Up at Marleigh," said Ginger. "He *might* be sens'ble enough to see that it's jus' as necess'ry for children to have improved conditions as what it is for grown-ups, but, of course," he ended gloomily, "he might not."

William folded up the document, slipped it into an envelope, wrote, "Outlaws Report. Pleese give to Parlyment" on the outside, and put it carefully into his pocket, then, accompanied by the other three Outlaws, made his way across the fields to Marleigh.

There, in front of a square Georgian house, stood a car laden with luggage.

"That's it," said Ginger excitedly. "That's where he lives an' he's goin' back to London today. His mother told mine he was."

A man with red tabs on the shoulders of his uniform hurried down to the car, threw a bag on to the top of the other bags and returned to the house.

He wore a lofty, supercilious expression, with a short moustache and an eyeglass.

"He looks high-up, all right," said William.

"But he doesn't look as if he'd take much notice of us," said Ginger, his excitement giving place to despondency.

"No, he doesn't," said William, inspecting him. "He doesn't look as if he'd even let us explain."

"He's got some jolly important papers with him," said Ginger. "He brought 'em home to go over, an' he's takin' them back with him today. I heard his mother tellin' mine that."

"*Gosh!*" said William excitedly. "*Tell* you what we could do! We could jus' slip our Report in with his papers an' it would go to the Government with them an' be made an Act of Parliament. That's a jolly good idea."

"But how're we goin' to slip it in with them?"

William surveyed the back of the car, piled up with cases and rugs.

"I bet they're somewhere there," he said. "I bet I could find them if I had a good look. I'll get in an' have a try, anyway."

With that, William crept up to the car, opened the door, and, crouching under a large rug that was hanging down untidily from the back seat, began his investigations among the cases that were piled there. Almost immediately Major Hamilton came down the garden path, leapt into the driving seat, waved his hand carelessly towards the house and started the car. It drove off, leaving the three remaining Outlaws staring after it, their faces petrified by horror.

William was only slightly perturbed. The car would be sure to stop somewhere for petrol or something, and then, having slipped his Report in among Major Hamilton's other important papers, he would make his way back as best he could. In fact, the element of adventure in the situation was rather exhilarating than otherwise ... Very quietly – so as not to attract the attention of the driver – he continued to burrow among the cases. A locked attaché-case seemed the most likely receptacle. Remembering the satchel of keys that he still carried over

THE CASE WAS FULL OF PAPERS THAT LOOKED IMPORTANT.

his shoulder, he took it off and searched among it. Several
keys seemed to be of suitable size. He tried them, one
after another. The last one fitted. He opened the case. Yes,
it was full of papers that looked important. He decided to
put the Outlaws' Report at the bottom, so that it should
be taken out with the others, and not attract attention till
it was presented to the Government along with them and,
with luck, made automatically into an Act of Parliament.

Turning the other papers out carelessly, he bundled them into his satchel, with a faint realisation of the fact that, though less important than the Report, they were still important, and must be kept carefully till they could be replaced in the attaché-case. He tried the Report in every position and at every angle, in order to find out which looked most impressive – right way up, with the words "Outlaws Report. Please Give to Parlyment"

boldly displayed... wrong way up... sideways...
cornerways...

Suddenly the car began to slow down. Concerned
for the safety of his precious manuscript, William hastily
locked the attaché-case, then, concerned for his own
safety, crouched beneath the rug...

The car stopped, and William, peeping from a corner
of the rug, saw that it had drawn up in front of a hotel.
Major Hamilton got out of the car and entered the
hotel. William considered his next step. He had done what
he had come to do, so he might as well return home
before he was discovered. The Report was now on its
way to the Government in London... and presumably
something would be done about it sooner or later.

Very cautiously, he slipped out of the car (on the side
away from the hotel) and set off down the road. He'd
probably find out where he was from a post office or
something. He might even be able to "hitch hike" home,
which would be a novel and enjoyable experience. A
motor-cyclist passed him, going at a breakneck speed.
William put out his hand to stop him, but received only
a scowl in reply. Oh well, probably something else would
pass him soon, and he'd try again.

He walked on for a short distance then stopped,
stunned by a sudden recollection. He'd still got Major
Hamilton's papers in his satchel. Gosh! He'd better take
them back again, or he'd be getting in a row with the
Government, and it might even put them against the
Outlaws' Report. He mustn't risk that... Hastily he
retraced his steps to the car. At the car he found Major
Hamilton and a man who was evidently the manager of
the hotel. Major Hamilton looked white and shaken.

194

"I was only in the hotel a minute or two," he was saying. "It was there on the seat of the car – a locked attaché-case – when I went in, and it's gone now. I must get in touch with the police at once."

"You didn't lock the car?" said the manager.

Major Hamilton grew paler than ever.

"I'd lost the key," he said. "I admit I took a chance. As I said, I wasn't in the hotel more than a minute or two and I thought I'd be able to see it from the window. I suppose that someone knew I'd got the papers and had been following me."

"What's been lost?" said William, pushing himself between them. "Your attaché-case?"

Major Hamilton looked at him, as if hoping against all reasonable hope that help might be forthcoming even from this unlikely source.

"Yes . . . Do you know anything about it? There were most important papers in it."

"I should think there were," said William indignantly. "There was our Report. Gosh! If *that's* been stolen . . ."

"What on earth are you talking about?" said the Major impatiently. "I'm speaking of important Government papers and . . ."

"Oh, them!" said William carelessly. "I've got *them* all right. I was jus' comin' to put 'em back."

With that, he slung off his satchel, took out the papers and thrust them into the astonished Major's hand.

"I've got a lot of keys, too," he continued calmly. "I bet I could find one to fit your car."

There were long explanations, at the end of which (a key was actually found to fit the car) the Major took him into the hotel, gave him a meal that seemed to William one of pre-war magnificence and saw him into a 'bus that would take him home.

"No, I didn't get it to London," explained William to the Outlaws. "It was stole before we got there."

"Gosh!" said the Outlaws, impressed. "I shouldn't have thought anyone knew enough about it for that."

"Oh well," admitted William, "there were some other papers, too, but I bet it was our Report they were after really. Someone must have found out about it . . ."

"Then we won't get an Act of Parliament?" said the Outlaws, disappointed.

"Well, p'raps not an Act of Parliament exactly," admitted William, "but this Major Hamilton says he'll do the best he can for us. He'll take us to a pantomime at Christmas."

The Outlaws' drooping spirits soared.

"A pantomime! *Gosh!*"

"*Hurrah!*"

For the Outlaws had acquired a certain philosophy of life and realised that a pantomime in the hand is worth a dozen Acts of Parliament in the bush . . .

CHAPTER NINE

WILLIAM AND THE AMERICAN TIE

"**W**ELL, WHAT'LL WE do now?" said Ginger. "We've done about everything you can do in a garden."

"An' some of the things you can't," said William with a certain modest pride.

The two sat on the roof of the tool-shed, surveying the garden beneath them. Rows of sagging runner beans bore witness to their journeys through the jungle as Red Indians, the herbaceous border showed traces of their forced landings as pilots from the branches of the copper beech that stretched above it, several stones had been dislodged from the rockery during their spirited attack and defence of a mountain fortress and the roller, after a short and inglorious career as a tank, had come to rest in the middle of the asparagus bed.

"Yes," added William thoughtfully, "p'r'aps we'd better go an' play somewhere else for a bit. I didn't re'lise that it – *showed* as much as what it does."

"P'r'aps it's 'cause w're lookin' at it from up there," said Ginger optimistically.

"Yes," said William, reassured by the explanation, "p'r'aps when you look at it flat it doesn't look so bad.

Anyway, let's get away for a bit an' give people time to find it an' forget about it before they see us again."

"Let's go an' make a camp-fire somewhere," said Ginger. "I've got some matches."

"No," said William. "Let's go to the wood an' try climbin' that tree again."

"All right," said Ginger, beginning to slither down the side of the tool-shed, "an' I bet we get to the top this time."

William let go his hold on the roof and rolled down to the ground, landing in the middle of a heap of potting soil that his father had carefully placed there the evening before. He stood up, brushing the soil from his person in a sketchy fashion.

"I bet we could make a sort of house in that tree if we got to the top," he said. "I'd like to go back to the days when people lived in trees. I think it ought to come back into fashion. People grumble 'cause they can't get houses, but they never seem to think of goin' back to trees. I bet trees'd be much more fun to live in than houses."

"It'd be jolly difficult gettin' the furniture up," said Ginger. "Sideboards an' pianos an' baths an' things – an' I bet they'd always be tumblin' out of them. It'd be jolly difficult to balance them on the branches."

"We wouldn't need furniture, you chump," said William. "We'd jus' live in the branches the same as the tree-dwellers did. I bet if we all went back to bein' tree-dwellers, we'd have a much jollier time than what we have now. We could graft apples an' gooseberries an' pears an' peaches an' grapes an' bananas an' pineapples on the trees for food an' jus' eat 'em when we felt like it 'stead of havin' to come in for meals. I'd be a jolly good grafter but my father never lets me get any practice."

"Gosh, yes!" said Ginger as the possibilities of the idea opened out before him. "An' we wouldn't have to do any homework 'cause there wouldn't be any tables or ink."

"An' we could stay up as long as we liked," said William, "'cause there wouldn't be any beds an' we needn't go to school 'cause I don't expect Ole Fathead can climb trees."

"Ole Fathead" was Mr Vastop – a master who had joined the staff of William's school for a term to replace Mr French, William's form master, while Mr French took a much needed holiday to recover from an operation – and, incidentally, from William. Between William and Mr French a feud had existed ever since their first meeting, but it was a feud run on established and almost friendly lines. They respected each other as foes and called an occasional truce in order to rally their forces and prepare for the next onslaught. But Mr Vastop – inevitably nick-named Old Fathead – was different. He was a rat-like man with a long, thin nose and a small, pursed mouth that showed sharply projecting teeth. He was bad-tempered and sarcastic and had an unpleasant habit of luring his victims by friendly overtures to make confidences that he could use as weapons against them when opportunity arose. He had even – smiling his rat-like smile – drawn from William confidences about his beloved mongrel Jumble, only to comment in public on William's likeness to his "ill-conditioned cur" when next William arrived at school in his usual state of dishevelment.

"Oh, let's not think about *him*," said William. "He's

not fit to live in a tree. A bog or a – a quicksand's where *he* ought to be. Anyway, it was sucks to him on Wednesday. Fancy thinkin' that Denis Compton played for Kent!"

Last Wednesday William had passed Mr Vastop holding forth with a knowledgeable air to a group of small boys and had corrected one of Mr Vastop's statements as he passed with perhaps unnecessary brusqueness. Mr Vastop's rat-like face had reddened, but William had vanished before he could think of an adequate rejoinder.

"He's jus' ign'rant," continued William contemptuously. "What's the use of him havin' all those letters after his name if he thinks that Denis Compton plays for Kent? He's the mos' ign'rant man I've ever met."

"Well, never mind him," said Ginger. "Let's get on with this tree house."

They skirted the side of the house and passed the open sitting-room window. Through the open window they had an unimpeded view of Robert and a girl with eyes of periwinkle blue sitting side by side on the settee. The girl was just handing Robert what appeared to be a tie of virulent colour and design.

"Gosh!" said William, putting his head in at the window in order to inspect the strange object at closer quarters.

"Get out!" thundered Robert.

William got out.

"Who is she?" said Ginger as they proceeded on their way.

"She's that girl that the family of's come to live at The Cedars," said William. "She's just got back from staying with some relations in America an' she's called

"GOSH!" EXCLAIMED WILLIAM, PUTTING HIS HEAD THROUGH
THE WINDOW.

some awful name I can't remember – something like rock cakes but a bit diff'rent – an' Robert says she's the mos' beautiful girl he's ever seen."

"She looked jolly ordin'ry to me," said Ginger.

"They all look jolly ordin'ry," said William, "but" – with rising excitement – "did you see that tie she was givin' him? I've never seen a tie like that before. It'd got people an' balls an' things all over it."

"Oh, never mind it," said Ginger. "Come on to the woods an' let's get goin' with the tree house."

In the sitting-room Robert winced and blenched as Roxana held the tie before his eyes.

"They're all the rage in New York," she said. "They're so much smarter than the dull ties people wear in England, aren't they?"

"Yes," said Robert, rallying his shattered forces.

"I chose it specially for you, Robert. I wanted to bring you something that would – well, that would be a sort of symbol of the bond between us. I wanted it to *mean* something. I'm funny like that, you know, Robert. I like things to *mean* something."

"Yes," agreed Robert, trying to hide his bewilderment. "Yes – er – quite."

"You see, it's modern," said Roxana earnestly. "It isn't stuffy and old-fashioned like spots and stripes and things. It belongs to the new world that you and I belong to – the world that isn't bound by the old conventions and ideas. I'm funny like that, you know, Robert. I can't bear old conventions and ideas. What I'm trying to say, Robert, is that it's more than just a tie."

Robert gazed at the stalwart, strangely accoutred figures of baseball players who, in various attitudes – springing, crouching, leaping, grovelling – adorned the strip of material. A ball appeared at intervals but without much indication as to what part it played in the nightmare gambol.

"Yes," said Robert, feeling himself on firmer ground. "Yes, I can see that it is."

"It's almost what one might call a *gage d'amour*, Robert." She threw him a melting glance from the periwinkle blue eyes. "You understand what that means, don't you?"

"Well," Robert gave a short nervous laugh and passed his hand along the inside of his collar. Roxana's French had been superbly Parisian and Robert's, like that of Chaucer's nun, belonged to the school of Stratford-atte-Bowe. "Well – er—"

"French, you know," said Roxana kindly.

"Oh, yes, that!" said Robert in a tone of relief. "Yes . . . I can't say it like you do" – reverently – "but I know what you mean now. It – it's wonderful of you, Roxana."

"It's a sort of *token*, Robert, that we share the same ideals, that the same things *mean* the same things to us, that we both want to throw overboard everything that's old-fashioned and out-of-date and – insular."

Robert looked at the tie again. It was growing on him. No one else in the village had anything to compare with it. It would, he felt, confer a certain distinction on him, raise him above the ruck of people who wore small spots and stripes round their collars. Already he heard himself saying in a tone of airy amusement: "Haven't you really seen one like this before? Oh, everyone wears them in New York."

"I'll put it on now, shall I?" he said, beginning to undo the sober length of navy and white rayon that enclosed his neck.

Roxana laid a hand on his arm.

"No, Robert. I want to make a sort of *occasion* of it. I'm funny like that, you know. When a thing means a lot to me I like to make a sort of *occasion* of it. You see, I'm having a party on Thursday for my friends – my own special friends – and I want you to come to it. And – perhaps it sounds silly but I'm funny like that – I want you to wear the tie then for the first time. If you come to the party wearing the tie it will be a sign that we're *real* friends, that you feel the same as I do about stuffiness and convention and that sort of thing. And if you don't—"

"But, Roxana, of course I do," said Robert earnestly. "Of course I'll wear the tie."

"Think it over, Robert. Think it over carefully. It means such a lot to both of us," said Roxana in a tone of deep solemnity. "Only last year—"

She stopped and her face darkened as at some painful memory.

"Yes, dear?" encouraged Robert.

"There was a man . . . He *seemed* to share all my ideas about that sort of thing and I went out to New York to stay with my cousins – just as I did this year – and I brought back a tie for him, just as I have done for you. It was like this but perhaps a little more daring" – Robert looked at the tie and blinked – "and I said to him just what I've said to you and told him to wear it at my party if he really felt for me what he said he felt for me and – and—"

"Yes?"

"He just didn't. He pretended he'd lost it. Did you ever hear of such a cowardly trick? He just didn't wear it and said he'd lost it. I never spoke to him again. I never looked at him again. He didn't *mean* anything any more. I'm funny like that, you know. Once a person lets me down they never mean anything to me any more."

"But of course I'll wear the tie at your party, Roxana," said Robert. "It's wonderful of you to ask me."

"It was such a *cowardly* excuse to say he'd lost it, wasn't it? I saw him then as he really was. I cut him right out of my life. You think I was right, don't you, Robert?"

"Indeed I do," said Robert fervently.

"And you won't wear it *before* the party, will you?"

"Of course not," said Robert. "As a matter of fact I couldn't wear it before because I'm going off on a few days' hiking holiday with Jameson tomorrow, and I shan't be back till Thursday afternoon, anyway."

Roxana heaved a long, deep sigh.

"I'm afraid I'm a rather complicated and unusual character, Robert," she said. "Not many people really understand me. That's the great tragedy of my life. I have very high ideals for my friends and so few of them come up to them ... I expect you think I'm very foolish, don't you, Robert?"

"I think you're adorable," said Robert, glad to have reached a point where he felt sure of his ground. "I think that everything about you's adorable – your eyes, your hair, your mouth and – well, I love your name, too. Roxana ... It's the most beautiful name I've ever heard in my life."

"Well, it's *me*, isn't it?" said Roxana. "As soon as I saw it – in some book, I've forgotten which – I knew it was me. My parents had me christened Elsie. I've tried to forgive them for it, but it hasn't been easy. I feel things so deeply. Elsie!" She shuddered. "It just isn't me at all, and if a thing isn't me I just can't put up with it. It seems to cramp my whole personality. I'm funny like that, Robert ... I was a little tempted by Perdita at one time, but as soon as I saw Roxana I knew it was me."

"Roxana ..." repeated Robert, lingering bemusedly over the syllables. "It's the most beautiful name I've ever heard in my life, and it suits you so."

"Well, it does show that I'm just a little out of the ordinary, doesn't it?"

205

"Out of the ordinary?" repeated Robert ardently. "Oh, Roxana, when first I saw you . . ."

The conversation continued on familiar lines.

The building of the house in the tree also continued on familiar lines.

William fell out of his tree and tore his shirt, got soaked to the skin in an effort to "lay on" water from the stream to his improvised "bedroom", lost both handkerchief and garters during the process of turning the top branch into a flagstaff, acquired a coating of soot in an attempt to build a fire in the "sitting-room" . . . and at last was chased from the wood – with Ginger close at his heels – by an infuriated keeper whose threats of vengeance added the final touch of colour to an already colourful morning.

"Gosh!" panted William when they had reached the safety of the main road. "He said some jolly int'restin' things this time, didn't he?"

"Yes," said Ginger. "He's thought out some fresh ones since las' time . . . You know, I dunno that trees are all that good as houses."

"Well, let's try a diff'rent sort nex' time," said William. "I bet that big fir tree would be better. Once you get started on fir trees they're jolly easy to climb."

"But there's not much room on the branches," said Ginger. "I bet that oak would be better."

"We'll try 'em both," said William, "an' we'll have to make a sort of lift for Jumble to get up it. I've tried to teach him to climb trees but he can't. He gets all muddled up with his legs."

"We could tie a rope round his middle an' jus' pull him up."

"Yes," agreed William but he spoke absently.

His thoughts were not with the tree house. They were with the tie that he had seen Roxana present to Robert.

"Gosh, wasn't it wizard!" he said. "Men playin' football all over it. I've never seen one like that before. Gosh! A *tie* with men playin' football all over it!"

"I didn't see it prop'ly," said Ginger, "but if it's American it mus' be baseball, not football."

"Well, baseball, then," said William. "I'll show it you if I get a chance. I know where he keeps his ties."

He described it to Henry and Douglas. He described it to the whole form. He found himself committed – before he quite realised it – to bringing the tie to school and displaying it at "break" the next day. He felt certain qualms about the undertaking, but Robert's absence on his hiking holiday seemed to make the risk comparatively negligible. I'll jus' take it there an' bring it back, he assured himself. If I jus' take it there an' bring it back, nothin' can happen to it . . ."

Cautiously, warily, he entered Robert's bedroom and opened the wardrobe door. There, on a string stretched across the back of the door, hung Robert's ties . . . but the new one was not among them. Robert had heard his mother casually mention a Jumble Sale that was to be held at the Women's Institute on the Saturday of his absence and, remembering the last occasion of a Women's Institute Jumble Sale, to which she had contributed an assortment of his most cherished possessions, he had found, as he thought, a safe and secret hiding-place for the precious tie at the bottom of a box of collars in the top drawer of his chest of drawers. And there, after an unsystematic but thorough search, William found it, still wrapped in tissue paper, carefully concealed in the cardboard box beneath the circle of collars.

He slipped it into his pocket and set off for school, where his highest expectations were fulfilled. His contemporaries crowded round him at "break", spellbound by the gaudiness and vigour of his exhibit. Rising to the occasion, William gave a spirited account of the game of baseball, invented on the spur of the moment.

"This one's tryin' to jump over that one an' this one's crawling along to get nearer the goal post an' this one's doin' a native war dance – it's part of the game – an' this one's—"

"Gosh! How many balls do they use?" said someone. William hastily counted them.

"Yes, they play with seven balls," he said. "It's part of the game."

The crowd gave a gasp of wonder and amazement.

"Oh, yes," said William, who was by this time carried a little beyond himself. "Seven balls is nothin' to them. You can play with as many balls as you like in baseball. You try an' hit one ball with another ball, same as you do in billiards . . ."

He realised that he was getting a little out of his depth and was relieved when, at this point, the bell rang and his audience swarmed indoors. But the whole thing had gone to his head. He had enjoyed holding forth to a spellbound audience as a baseball authority and he wanted to go on doing it. Several other imaginary features of the game had occurred to him. He nudged Frankie

"GIVE THAT TO ME, BROWN," SAID MR VASTOP.

Parker, who sat at the next desk, and took the tie from his pocket again.

"Look, Frankie," he whispered. "This one with his mouth open's the captain an' he's doin' the native war cry. It goes like this—"

The sharp thin hand of Mr Vastop descended on his shoulder, and the sharp thin voice of Mr Vastop cut into the first whispered notes of the war cry.

"Give that to me, Brown."

And Mr Vastop strode back to his desk, bearing the captured tie with an air of triumph.

"Our friend Brown has a somewhat flashy taste in ties," he said, holding it at arm's length and inspecting it with his rat-like sneer. "A taste that should not be encouraged in one so young. A good thing, perhaps, that he will not now have the opportunity of disporting himself in this particular specimen."

The lid of Mr Vastop's desk closed over the tie and horror closed over William. He did not know about Roxana's party and Robert's solemn undertaking to wear the tie for that occasion, but he knew that the tie was a present to Robert from Roxana, he knew that his inspection of the tie through the open window had betrayed his interest in it, he knew that Robert would instantly connect its disappearance with that interest . . . and he knew that retribution at the hands of Robert would be swift and sure.

"It's all right," he assured his friends after class with a confidence he did not feel. "I'll tell him it's Robert's. He'll let me have it back all right if I tell him it's Robert's. I – I'll jus' have a word with him at the end of school."

"I bet he'll be mad," said Ginger, "an' I bet he'll say you can't have it back till the end of term."

William's friends watched William having a word with Mr Vastop at the end of school. Mr Vastop was not mad. Mr Vastop was, on the contrary, delighted. Mr Vastop considered that William had "shown him up" in the matter of the cricketer and he never forgave anyone who showed him up. He welcomed the opportunity of getting even with William and intended to make full use of it.

William's usually ruddy countenance had paled a little by the time he rejoined his friends.

"Gosh!" he said. "He say's he's not goin' to give it me back at all. I told him it was Robert's an' he didn't care. I told him I'd get in an awful row with Robert an' he didn't care about that either. I told him Robert'd be mad with him an' – gosh! – he didn't even seem to care

about that. I said he could do anythin' he liked to me –
he could *torcher* me if he liked – if only he'd let me have
it back. I said he could pull my teeth out an' screw my
thumbs same as they used to do to people in hist'ry."

"An' what did he say to that?" said Ginger.

"He said that mental torture was much more effective
an' that he'd enjoy watchin' me undergo it an' that he
hoped Robert would apply the other sort of torture to
me . . . an' I bet he will, too!"

"Well, there isn't anythin' you can do about it, is
there?" said Ginger.

William frowned thoughtfully.

"There's nearly a week before Robert comes back. I
might try somethin' . . ."

"What can you try?"

"I'll try meltin' his heart first," said William after a
slight pause. "He's a villain all right, but lots of villains
get their hearts melted in books an' I don't see why he
shouldn't get his melted. Even a villain's got a better self
an' I'm jolly well goin' to try 'n' find his."

But William's search was unrewarded. He produced
a geography exercise that, except for a few blots and
several wild misstatements, was as perfect as he could
well make it. He spent a whole evening learning history
dates, which he repeated, with only a pardonable degree
of inaccuracy, the next day. He picked up a pencil that
Mr Vastop had dropped and presented it to him, teeth
bared in a polite smile. He even, when Mr Vastop joined
the spectators of the Saturday afternoon cricket match,
moved forward a chair for him, resisting a strong temptation to draw it back just as Mr Vastop was sitting
down . . . and Mr Vastop received all these attentions with

a rat-like smile that showed the deep pleasure he took in the situation. The days slipped by till Wednesday, the eve of Robert's return.

"Well, he's not got a better self," said William firmly. "I've tried to find one an' he jus' hasn't got one. He's one of those villains without a better self, same as Hitler an' Nero an' that man at the Income Tax my father's always talkin' about. I'll have to do somethin' desp'rate. With Robert comin' back tomorrow it'll *have* to be somethin' desp'rate."

"Gosh!" said Ginger. "You aren't goin' to kidnap him or anythin', are you?"

William considered the suggestion with interest and abandoned it reluctantly.

"N-no, I don't think so. It'd take too long to fix up an' I wouldn't know where to keep him an' there'd be an awful row about it when he came out."

"What're you goin' to do, then?" said Ginger.

"I'm goin' to get it back," said William. "He's taken it out of his desk 'cause I've looked, so it mus' be in his house. I'm goin' to wait till there's no one in his house, an' then I'm goin' to go in an' fetch it."

"Gosh! You could get put in prison for that," said Ginger.

"Well, I shouldn't mind goin' to prison as long as I'd got that tie back first. I don't s'pose they'd put me in prison straight away. I heard someone say that prisons are jolly full up nowadays, so I 'spect people have got to wait their turn same as they have to for hospitals. Anyway, if I was in prison I'd miss his rotten ole hist'ry an' geography lessons. An' I could always escape when I'd had enough of it. I've always wanted to try escapin' from prison. I'd saw through the bars an' let myself down by tyin' my sheets together an' then I'd—"

It was clear that William was in danger of being carried away by his theme, so Ginger hastily interrupted:

"Yes, but about that tie . . ."

"Oh, yes," said William, reluctantly tearing himself from the mental contemplation of his daring escape from prison and returning to the matter in hand. "Yes, about the tie . . . Well, we'll go to his house, same as I said, an' wait till he's gone out an' – well – jus' go in an' take it. I bet he'll leave a window open. People always do. An' if he doesn't I bet I can climb up by that shed an' get in by an upstairs window, same as I do for my mother when she forgets her key."

"S'pose there's a charwoman or someone there?"

"There won't be. Ole Fathead's got ole Frenchie's house an' ole Frenchie's charwoman, an' she only goes there in the morning."

"When'll we do it?"

"Today, of course. It's a matter of life an' death. If we don't do it today we're ru'ned. At least I am. When Robert's mad he sticks at nothin' . . . Let's go home for tea an' then go round to Ole Fathead's an' do it."

Mr Vastop, sallying forth from his house an hour later, did not notice the two small boys who lurked in the shadow of the hedge on the other side of the road.

"Come on, quick!" said William, as the small dapper figure vanished from view. "There's a window open. I bet it won't take two minutes to get in an' find that tie an' get out again."

Luck seemed to be with them. The road was empty and remained empty as they raised the window sash and entered the little sitting-room of Mr French's house, now in the temporary possession of Mr Vastop.

"Ole Frenchie used to keep things he confiscated in this drawer," said William, opening a drawer in the bureau. "He's often given me things back out of it when I've pleaded with him. He's a villain, same as Ole Fathead, but he's got a better self."

A thorough search of the drawer, however, revealed only neat stacks of notepaper and envelopes . . . boxes of paper clips . . . coloured pencils . . . a tin of throat lozenges . . . copies of Mr Vastop's testimonials, which William read with incredulous surprise, and a photograph of Mr Vastop himself, to which William could not resist adding a turned-up moustache, an enormous pipe and a feathered hat.

"S' not there," he said at last, slamming the drawer back into place. "Let's try that cupboard."

"You're makin' an awful noise, banging about," said Ginger. "I bet someone'll hear from the road an' come in to see what's happ'nin."

William looked round the room.

"All right, let's turn the wireless on," he said. "I bet no one'll wonder what's happ'nin' if they hear the wireless on."

He switched on the knob and the strains of a military band filled the room.

"We mus' leave things tidy, too," said Ginger a little nervously. "We'll get in an awful row if he finds out we've been."

"All right," said William, carefully replacing a pile of old magazines in the cupboard and resisting the temptation to sample a tin of biscuits that reposed beneath them. "Let's try that chest of drawers over there now."

The search continued. The military band gave place to a play that seemed to consist chiefly of a dialogue between two men. The cupboard and chest of drawers were explored without success. It was just as they were on the point of reluctantly abandoning the search that Ginger gave a gasp and said:

"He's comin' back, William. He's jus' openin' the gate."

"Gosh!" said William. "Let's hide quick!"

Ginger dived behind the cupboard, William behind a large arm-chair. From his hiding-place William saw Mr Vastop enter the gate jauntily, then stop and grow pale as the voices of the radio dialogue – lowered at a dramatic point of the plot – reached him through the open window. He stood there, staring at the house, his rat-like mouth drawn into a grin of terror. Then he started back to the gate. Frankie Parker was passing along the road.

"Parker!" squeaked Mr Vastop in a high-pitched agitated voice. "Run to the police station at once and tell them to send someone here quickly. Say that I've come back from the village to find burglars in the house. Hurry! Hurry! Hurry!"

"Yes, sir," said Frankie and set off at a decorous trot down the road. Nothing had ever been known to ruffle Frankie's composure.

As Mr Vastop still stood gazing in fascinated horror at the house, the voices of the actors died away and the announcer's voice, clear and resonant, floated out to him.

"That was *Peril of Life*, a play by Adrian Ashtead . . .

The time is now half-past five ... We present Donald Macalastair's Dance Band ..."

There followed the lilting strains of a dance band.

Mr Vastop's mouth dropped open to its fullest extent. His eyes goggled ... He ran to the front door, unlocked it and entered the sitting-room. There he stood, gazing at the wireless, his mouth opening and shutting distractedly.

"Oh, dear! Oh, dear!" he jibbered. "I must have left it on after tea. I quite thought I'd turned it off. Oh, dear! Oh, dear!"

He took out his handkerchief and mopped his brow. Then, as if coming to a sudden decision, he switched off the knob ... opened the drawers of his bureau and tossed their contents on the floor ... twisted his tie awry, rumpled his hair, pulled his shirt about ... overthrew a small chair ... kicked the hearth-rug to one side ... scattered a few objects from the chimney-piece on to the hearth and emptied the contents of a small bookcase over the carpet. He had just completed these preparations when the stalwart figure of the policeman appeared at the gate and made its majestic way up to the front door.

"Come in, Constable," called Mr Vastop, panting noisily. "You're just too late. I dealt with the fellows as best I could, but I'm afraid they got away. Here's the battlefield."

He waved his hand in a sweeping gesture round the disordered room.

"Blimey!" said the policeman, surveying the scene and taking his notebook from his pocket. "Perhaps you'll tell me just what happened, sir?"

"Certainly, Constable, certainly," said Mr Vastop. "I heard the fellows' voices and caught a glimpse of them through the window as I came in at the gate, so I sent a boy who was passing to fetch you and came in myself to do the best I could without you. I found two men here just turning out the contents of the bureau, as you see."

"Yes, sir . . . Could you describe them, sir?"

"Certainly, Constable, certainly . . . Both were large men. One was dark, in a dark suit, and the other was – er – fair, in a light suit. I closed with them at once so naturally I hadn't time to notice many details."

"Of course, sir," said the policeman, writing busily.

"I knocked the first one down, but the other then closed with me, and, while I was dealing with him, the first one got up. I managed to get to the door and hoped to hold them till you came. I gave the fair one a blow that sent him reeling against the bookcase, knocking the books out, as you see, and then I had a struggle with both of them together in which I certainly didn't come off worst. I think" – he gave his short sarcastic laugh – "that you'll find one with a broken nose and the other with a dislocated jaw."

"You certainly showed some pluck, sir," said the policeman respectfully.

Mr Vastop repeated his short sarcastic laugh.

"Oh, well . . . I may be lacking in many good qualities, but I flatter myself that I am not deficient in courage . . . The two of them got away at last, however, and, I'm afraid, have made good their escape."

The policeman looked at the contents of the bureau, strewn about the room.

"Much missing, sir?" he said.

"Fortunately not," said Mr Vastop. "Nothing missing, as a matter of fact. They hadn't really started on the job

"YOU CERTAINLY SHOWED SOME PLUCK, SIR," SAID THE
POLICEMAN.

when I disturbed them – and I think that 'disturb' is the
right word. Ha, ha!"

"You can't describe them more fully, sir?" said the
policeman.

"Oh, yes, I think I can," said Mr Vastop, whose
imagination had had time for a little exercise in the
interval. "The dark one had a heavy moustache and – er
– a bulbous nose ... and the fair one was – er – going
slightly bald over one temple with – er – with bulbous
eyes. They were both villainous-looking men. Real gang-
ster types."

"You've come out of it very well, sir," said the
policeman. "I must say, I congratulate you on your

courage . . . Well, I'll get back with my report now. We *may* be able to catch them, but they've probably got clear into the woods by now and there's no telling what direction they'll take from there. Good-bye for the present, sir."

"Good-bye, Constable," said Mr Vastop, showing his sharp projecting teeth in an effusive smile, "and I'll hold myself ready for further questioning, of course. Ha, ha!"

The policeman took his majestic departure and Mr Vastop set to work, putting the room to rights. It was while he was picking up the ornaments from the hearth that he suddenly caught sight of William crouching behind the chair. He stared at him in horrified amazement. Once more his mouth dropped open and his eyes bulged.

"How dare you!" he sputted. "How *dare* you! What do you mean by it!" His thin arm darted out and dragged William from his hiding-place. "What do you mean by trespassing in my private room! I'll – I'll—"

"I came 'cause I wanted that tie you took off me," said William simply.

"We've not done any harm," said Ginger, emerging from his hiding-place. "We've only looked for it."

"I shall report you both to the Headmaster," said Mr Vastop. "I'll get you both expelled. I'll—" He stopped short and a thoughtful look came into his face. "How long have you been here?"

"All the time," said William. He spoke in a tone of guileless innocence. His face was devoid of expression. "We were here when you came in and turned the wireless off."

"We were here when you started upsetting the room," said Ginger.

"We were here when the policeman came," said William.

Mr Vastop stood looking at them. An ashen hue had invaded his cheeks. His rats' teeth shot out in a ghastly smile.

"You probably completely misunderstood the situation, my boys," he said. "Completely misunderstood it. It was – it was—" His face was contorted with effort as he searched for an explanation . . . then inspiration came and his teeth shot out again. "It was a wager. Yes, that was it. A wager. A wager I'd had with a friend. He bet me that I couldn't get away with it and I bet him that I could. You understand, don't you boys? Just a wager. A bet. A sort of joke. Ha, ha!"

"Yes," said William. His face was still a bland expressionless mask. "We'll 'splain that when we tell people about it, shall we?"

"WE WERE HERE WHEN THE POLICEMAN CAME," SAID WILLIAM.

"No, no," said Mr Vastop with a snarl that was evidently intended to be a conciliatory laugh. "Oh no, no, no! You mustn't tell anyone. It would be – it would be betraying my friend's confidence for you to tell anyone about it. I – I – I gave my friend my word that no one should know about it. I depend on your honour to say nothing of this to anyone."

William's face was now so expressionless that his homely features might have been hacked out of wood. He stared glassily in front of him.

"I've got a very bad mem'ry," he said. "It's a funny thing but I've got a sort of feeling that if you gave me back that tie of Robert's I wouldn't be able to remember anything else. It'd drive everything else clean out of my head."

Mr Vastop's face darkened.

"I told you—" he began severely, then stopped. "It's in my bedroom," he went on. "I'll get it."

He went from the room. William turned his expressionless face to Ginger and slowly lowered one eyelid. Mr Vastop returned, holding the tie, still wrapped in tissue paper, in his hand. He had recovered something of his poise.

"As you appear to be sorry for your disgraceful behaviour," he said, "I am willing to overlook it this once and let you have the – er – the confiscated article back. But I hope that this will be a lesson to you."

"Yes, sir," said William woodenly.

"And I take it that you will – er – respect my friend's confidence?"

"You mean, not tell anyone?" said William. "No, we won't tell anyone now we've got the tie back."

Mr Vastop heaved a sigh of relief. William, he knew, had almost every other conceivable failing, but he was not a boy who broke his word. He handed the tie back to William. William slipped it into his pocket, and the two boys set off down the road. Mr Vastop, standing at the window to watch their departure, once more took out his handkerchief and mopped his brow.

Cautiously, silently, William and Ginger made their way up to Robert's bedroom and opened the drawer where the collar box had been. The collar box was no longer there.

"Gosh!" said William. "What's happened to it?"

"Never mind," said Ginger. "Stick the thing anywhere and let's get away quick. I'm sick of this ole tie business. I want to get back to tree climbing. I want to try that fir tree."

"All right," said William. "I'll stick it here under his handkerchiefs. I bet he'll make a fuss about it when he comes home, anyway."

And Robert did make a fuss about it when he came home.

Arriving barely in time to change for Roxana's party, he dashed upstairs, his face glowing with happy antici-pation, then dashed downstairs, his face set in lines of horror.

"Mother, where's that box of collars that was in the top drawer of my chest of drawers?"

Mrs Brown looked up placidly from her mending.

"I sent it to the Jumble Sale, dear," she said.

"You sent it—"

Robert's voice failed him.

"Yes, dear. It was the box of collars that Aunt Maggie sent you for Christmas last year, wasn't it, and you said that they were a size too large. I remember that you said they were a size too large and I don't believe in hoarding things one can't use. Better let someone else have the use of them."

"But underneath the collars in the box..." said Robert hoarsely. "Didn't you look underneath the collars in the box?"

"No, dear," said Mrs Brown. "Why should I? I just sent the box as it was."

"Great Heavens!" said Robert wildly, as the full force of the tragedy struck him. "She'll never believe ... she'll *never* believe ..."

"Who'll never believe what, dear?" said Mrs Brown, breaking off a length of thread and holding her needle up to the light.

Robert gave a bitter laugh.

"Well, I only hope you'll never know what you've done to me," he said. "I only hope—" He noticed William hovering in the doorway and turned on him savagely. "Don't stand there listening to what doesn't concern you. Clear off!"

"Have you looked under your handkerchiefs, Robert?" said William innocently.

"Have I—?" began Robert in a voice of thunder, then stopped suddenly and took the stairs three at a time.

In a few seconds he returned, carrying the tie. William and Ginger were just going out of the front door.

"Yes, it was there," said Robert.

"I thought it might be," said William. "Come on, Ginger."

"Here! One minute!" said Robert, his mind a turmoil of relief, suspicion and bewilderment.

"'Fraid we've got to go," said William from the gate. "We want to make a tree house. We've wasted a lot of time already."

Robert stared after them as they ran down the road, his mind wrestling with the inexplicable disappearance and reappearance of the tie. He'd bet anything the little blighters knew something about it. Now he came to think of it, everything in his drawer looked as if it had been messed about. He hesitated, wondering whether to run after them and force the truth out of them; then decided to let things rest as they were. Where William was concerned it was often safer to let things rest as they were. He'd got the tie back and that was all that mattered. And there was no more time to be lost ... Standing in front of the hall mirror, he fastened the lurid strip round his neck; then, a beatific smile on his face, set off briskly for Roxana's party.

CHAPTER TEN

WILLIAM AND THE SCHOOL REPORT

IT WAS THE last day of term. The school had broken up, and William was making his slow and thoughtful way homeward. A casual observer would have thought that William alone among the leaping, hurrying crowd was a true student, that William alone regretted the four weeks of enforced idleness that lay before him. He walked draggingly and as if reluctantly, his brow heavily furrowed, his eyes fixed on the ground. But it was not the thought of the four weeks of holiday that was worrying William. It was a suspicion, amounting almost to a certainty, that he wasn't going to have the four weeks of holiday.

The whole trouble had begun with William's headmaster – a man who was in William's eyes a blend of Nero and Judge Jeffreys and the Spanish Inquisitioners, but who was in reality a harmless inoffensive man, anxious to do his duty to the youth entrusted to his care. William's father had happened to meet him in the train going up to town, and had asked him how William was getting on. The headmaster had replied truthfully and sadly that William didn't seem to be getting on at all. He hadn't, he said, the true scholar's zest for knowledge, his writing was atrocious and he didn't seem able to spell the simplest word or do the simplest sum. Then, brightening, he suggested that William should have coaching during the holidays. Mr Parkinson, one of the Junior form masters who lived near the school, would be at home for the four weeks, and had offered to coach backward boys. An hour a day. It would do William, said the headmaster enthusiastically, all the good in the world. Give him, as it were, an entirely new start. Nothing like individual coaching. Nothing at all. William's father was impressed. He saw four peaceful weeks during which William, daily occupied with his hour of coaching and its complement of homework, would lack both time and spirit to spread around him that devastation that usually marked the weeks of the holiday. He thanked the headmaster profusely, and said that he would let him know definitely later on.

William, on being confronted with the suggestion, was at first speechless with horror. When he found speech it was in the nature of a passionate appeal to all the powers of justice and fair dealing.

"In the *holidays*," he exclaimed wildly. "There's *lors* against it. I'm sure there's *lors* against it. I've never heard of *anyone* having lessons in the holidays. Not *anyone*! I bet even *slaves* didn't have lessons in the holidays. I bet if they knew about it in Parliament, there'd be an inquest about it. Besides I shall only get ill with overworkin' an' get brain fever same as they do in books, an' then you'll have to pay doctors' bills an' p'raps," darkly, "you'll have to pay for my funeral too I don't see how *anyone* could go on workin' like that for months an' *months* without ever stoppin' once an' not get brain fever and die of it. Anyone'd think you *wanted* me to die. An' if I did die I shun't be surprised if the judge did something to you about it."

His father, unmoved by this dark hint, replied, coolly, "I'm quite willing to risk it."

"An' I don't like Mr Parkinson," went on William gloomily, "he's always cross."

"Perhaps I can arrange it with one of the others," said Mr Brown.

"I don't like any of them," said William, still more gloomily, "they're all always cross."

He contemplated his wrongs in silence for a few minutes, then burst out again passionately:

"'T'isn't as if you weren't makin' me pay for that window. It's not fair payin' for it *an'* havin' lessons in the holidays."

"It's nothing to do with the window," explained Mr Brown wearily.

"I bet it is," said William darkly. "What else is it if it's not for the window? I've not done anythin' else lately."

"It's because your work at school fails to reach a high scholastic standard," said Mr Brown in a tone of ironical politeness.

"How d'you know?" said William after a moment's thought. "How d'you know it does? You've not seen my report. We don't get 'em till the last day."

"Your headmaster told me so."

"Ole Markie?" said William. "Well," indignantly, "I like that. I *like* that. He doesn't teach me at all. He doesn't teach me anythin' at all. I bet he was jus' makin' it up for somethin' to say to you. He'd got to say somethin' an' he couldn't think of anythin' else to say. I bet he tells everyone he meets that their son isn't doing well at school jus' for somethin' to say. I bet he's got a sort of habit of saying it to everyone he meets an' does it without thinkin'."

"All right," said William's father firmly, "I'll make no arrangements till I've seen your report. If it's a better one than it usually is, of course, you needn't have coaching."

William felt relieved. There were four weeks before the end of the term. Anything might happen. His father might forget about it altogether. Mr Parkinson might develop some infectious disease. It was even possible, though William did not contemplate the possibility with any confidence, that his report might be better. He carefully avoided any reference to the holidays in his father's hearing. He watched Mr Parkinson narrowly for any signs of incipient illness, rejoicing hilariously one morning when Mr Parkinson appeared with what seemed at first to be a rash but turned out on closer inspection to be shaving cuts. He even made spasmodic effort to display intelligence and interest in class, but his motive in asking questions was misunderstood, and taken to be his usual one of entertaining his friends or holding up the course of the lesson, and he relapsed into his usual state of boredom, lightened by surreptitious games with Ginger. And now the last day of the term had come, and the prospect of holiday coaching loomed ominously ahead. His father had not forgotten. Only last night he had reminded William that it depended on his report whether or not he was to have lessons in the holidays. Mr Parkinson looked almost revoltingly healthy, and in his pocket William carried the worst report he had ever had. Disregarding (in common with the whole school) the headmaster's injunction to give the report to his parents without looking at it first, he had read it apprehensively in the cloak-room and it had justified his blackest fears. He had had wild notions of altering it. The word "poor" could, he thought, easily be changed to "good", but few of the remarks stopped at "poor", and such additions as "Seems to take no interest at all in this subject" and "Work consistently ill prepared" would read rather oddly after the comment "good."

William walked slowly and draggingly. His father would demand the report, and at once make arrangements for the holiday coaching. The four weeks of the holidays stretched – an arid desert – before him.

"But one hour a day can't spoil the whole holidays, William," his mother had said, "you can surely spare one hour out of twelve to improving your mind."

William had retorted that for one thing his mind didn't need improving, and anyway it was *his* mind and he was quite content with it as it was, and for another, one hour a day *could* spoil the whole holidays.

"It can spoil it *absolutely*," he had protested. "It'll just make every single day of it taste of school. I shan't be able to enjoy myself any of the rest of the day after an hour of ole Parkie an' sums an' things. It'll spoil every *minute* of it."

"Well, dear," Mrs Brown had said with a sigh, "I'm sorry, but your father's made up his mind."

William's thoughts turned morosely to that conversation as he fingered the long envelope in his pocket. There didn't seem to be any escape. If he destroyed the report and pretended that he had lost it, his father would only write to the school for another, and they'd probably make the next one even more damning to pay him out for giving them extra trouble. The only possibility of escape was for him to have some serious illness, and that, William realised gloomily, would be as bad as the coaching.

To make things worse an aunt of his father's (whom William had not seen for several years) was coming over for the day, and William considered that his family was always more difficult to deal with when there were visitors. Having reached the road in which his home was, he halted irresolute. His father was probably coming home for lunch because of the aunt. He might be at home now. The moment when the report should be demanded was, in William's opinion, a moment to be postponed as far as possible. He needn't go home just yet. He turned aside into a wood, and wandered on aimlessly, still sunk in gloomy meditation, dragging his toes in the leaves.

"If ever I get into Parliament," he muttered fiercely, "I'll pass a *lor* against reports."

He turned a bend in the path and came face to face with an old lady. William felt outraged by the sight of her – old ladies had no right to be in woods – and was about to pass her hurriedly when she accosted him.

"I'm afraid I've lost my way, little boy," she said breathlessly. "I was directed to take a short cut from the station to the village through the wood, and I think I must have made a mistake."

William looked at her in disgust. She was nearly half a mile from the path that was a short cut from the station to the village.

"What part of the village d'you want to get to?" he said curtly.

231

"Mr Brown's house," said the old lady, "I'm expected there for lunch."

The horrible truth struck William. This was his father's aunt, who was coming over for the day. He was about to give her hasty directions, and turn to flee from her, when he saw that she was peering at him with an expression of delighted recognition.

"But it's William," she said. "I remember you quite well. I'm your Aunt Augusta. What a good thing I happened to meet you, dear! You can take me home with you."

William was disconcerted for a moment. They were in reality only a very short distance from his home. A path led from the part of the wood where they were across a field to the road where the Browns' house stood. But it was no part of William's plan to return home at once. He'd decided to put off his return as far as possible, and he wasn't going to upset his arrangements for the sake of anyone's aunt, much less his father's.

He considered the matter in frowning silence for a minute, then said:

"All right. You c'n come along with me."

"Thank you, my dear boy," said the old lady brightening. "Thank you. That will be *very* nice. I shall quite enjoy having a little talk with you. It's several years since I met you, but, of course, I recognised you at once."

William shot a suspicious glance at her, but it was evident that she intended no personal insult. She was smiling at him benignly.

She discoursed brightly as William led her further and further into the heart of the wood and away from his home. She told him stories of her far off childhood, describing in great detail her industry and obedience and perseverance and love of study. She had evidently been a shining example to all her contemporaries.

"There's no joy like the joy of duty done, dear boy," she said. "I'm sure that *you* know that."

"Uh-huh," said William shortly.

As they proceeded on into the wood, however, she grew silent and rather breathless.

"Are we – nearly there, dear boy?" she said.

They had almost reached the end of the wood, and another few minutes would have brought them out into the main road, where a 'bus would take them to within a few yards of William's home. William still had no intention of going home, and he felt a fierce resentment against his companion. Her chatter had prevented his giving his whole mind to the problem that confronted him. He felt sure that there was a solution if only he could think of it.

He sat down abruptly on a fallen tree and said casually:

"I'm afraid we're lost. We must've took the wrong turning. This wood goes on for miles an' miles. People've sometimes been lost for days."

"With – with no food?" said Aunt Augusta faintly.

"Yes, with no food."

"B-but, they must have died surely?"

"Yes," said William, "quite a lot of 'em were dead when they found 'em."

Aunt Augusta gave a little gasp of terror.

William's heart was less stony than he liked to think. Her terror touched him and he relented.

"Look here," he said, "I think p'raps that path'll get us out. Let's try that path."

"No," she panted. "I'm simply exhausted. I can't walk another step just now. Besides it might only take us further into the heart of the wood."

"Well, I'll go," said William. "I'll go an' see if it leads to the road."

"No, you *certainly* mustn't," said Aunt Augusta sharply, "we must at all costs keep together. You'll miss your way and we shall both be lost separately. I've read of that happening in books. People lost in forests and one going on to find the way and losing the others. No, I'm certainly not going to risk that. I *forbid* you going a yard without me, William, and I'm too much exhausted to walk any more just at present."

William, who had by now tired of the adventure and was anxious to draw it to an end as soon as possible, hesitated, then said vaguely:

"Well . . . s'pose I leave some sort of trail same as they do in books."

"But what can you leave a trail of?" said Aunt Augusta.

Suddenly William's face shone as if illuminated by a light within. He only just prevented himself from turning a somersault into the middle of a blackberry bush.

"I've got an envelope in my pocket," he said. "I'll tear that up. I mean—" he added cryptically, "it's a case of life and death, isn't it?"

"Do be careful then, dear boy," said Aunt Augusta anxiously. "Drop it every *inch* of the way. I hope it's something you can spare, by the way?"

"Oh yes," William assured her, "it's something I can spare all right."

He took the report out of his pocket, and began to

"S'POSE I LEAVE A TRAIL," SAID WILLIAM, "SAME AS THEY DO
IN BOOKS?"

tear it into tiny fragments. He walked slowly down the path, dropping the pieces, and taking the precaution of tearing each piece into further fragments as he dropped it. There must be no possibility of its being rescued and put together again. Certain sentences, for instance the one that said, "Uniformly bad. Has made no progress at all," he tore up till the paper on which they were written was almost reduced to its component elements.

The path led, as William had known it would, round a corner and immediately into the main road. He returned a few minutes later, having assumed an expression of intense surprise and delight.

"S'all right," he announced, "the road's jus' round there."

Aunt Augusta took out a handkerchief and mopped her brow.

"I'm so glad, dear boy," she said. "So very glad. What a relief! I was just wondering how one told edible from inedible berries. We might, as you said, have been here for days . . . Now let's just sit here and rest a few minutes before we go home. Is it far by the road?"

"No," said William. "There's a 'bus that goes all the way."

He took his seat by her on the log, trying to restrain the exuberant expansiveness of his grin. His fingers danced a dance of triumph in his empty pockets.

"I was so much relieved, dear boy," went on Aunt Augusta, "to see you coming back again. It would have been so terrible if we'd lost each other. By the way, what was the paper that you tore up, dear? Nothing important, I hope?"

William had his face well under control by now.

"It was my school report," he said, "I was jus' takin' it home when I met you."

He spoke sorrowfully as one who has lost his dearest treasure.

Aunt Augusta's face registered blank horror.

"You – you tore up your school report?" she said faintly.

"I had to," said William. "I'd rather," he went on, assuming an expression of noble self-sacrifice, "I'd rather lose my school report than have you starve to death."

It was clear that, though Aunt Augusta was deeply touched by this, her horror still remained.

"But – your school report, dear boy," she said. "It's dreadful to think of your sacrificing that for me. I remember so well the joy and pride of the moment when I handed my school report to my parents. I'm sure you know that moment well."

William, not knowing what else to do, heaved a deep sigh.

"Was it," said Aunt Augusta, still in a tone of deep concern and sympathy, "was it a *specially* good one?"

"We aren't allowed to look at them," said William unctuously; "they always tell us to take them straight home to our parents without looking at them."

"Of course. Of course," said Aunt Augusta. "Quite right, of course, but – oh, how disappointing for you, dear boy. You have some idea no doubt what sort of a report it was?"

"Oh yes," said William, "I've got some sort of an idea all right."

"And I'm sure, dear," said Aunt Augusta, "that it was a very, very good one."

237

William's expression of complacent modesty was rather convincing.

"Well . . . I – I dunno," he said self-consciously.

"I'm sure it was," said Aunt Augusta. "I know it was. And *you* know it was really. I can tell that, dear boy, from the way you speak of it."

"Oh . . . I dunno," said William, intensifying the expression of complacent modesty that was being so successful. "I dunno . . ."

"And that tells me that it was," said Aunt Augusta triumphantly, "far more plainly than if you said it was. I like a boy to be modest about his attainments. I don't like a boy to go about boasting of his successes in school. I'm sure you never do that, do you, dear boy?"

"Oh no," said William with perfect truth. "No, I never do that."

"But I'm so worried about the loss of your report. How quietly and calmly you sacrificed it." It was clear that her appreciation of William's nobility was growing each minute. "Couldn't we try to pick up the bits on our way to the road and piece them together for your dear father to see?"

"Yes," said William. "Yes, we could try'n' do that."

He spoke brightly, happy in the consciousness that he had torn up the paper into such small pieces that it couldn't possibly be put together.

"Let's start now, dear, shall we?" said Aunt Augusta; "I'm quite rested."

They went slowly along the little path that led to the road.

Aunt Augusta picked up the "oo" of "poor" and said, "This must be a 'good' of course," and she picked up the "ex" of "extremely lazy and inattentive" and said, "This must be an 'excellent' of course," but even Aunt Augusta realised that it would be impossible to put together all the pieces.

"I'm afraid it can't be done, dear," she said sadly. "How *disappointing* for you. I feel so sorry that I mentioned it at all. It must have raised your hopes."

"No, it's quite all right," said William, "it's quite all right. I'm not disappointed. Really I'm not."

"I *know* what you're feeling, dear boy," said Aunt Augusta. "I know what I should feel myself in your place. And I hope – I *hope* that I'd have been as brave about it as you are."

William, not knowing what to say, sighed again. He was beginning to find his sigh rather useful. They had reached the road now. A 'bus was already in sight. Aunt Augusta hailed it, and they boarded it together. They completed the journey to William's house in silence. Once Aunt Augusta gave William's hand a quick surreptitious pressure of sympathy and whispered:

"I know *just* what you are feeling, dear boy."

William, hoping that she didn't, hastily composed his features to their expression of complacent modesty, tinged with deep disappointment – the expression of a boy who has had the misfortune to lose a magnificent school report.

His father was at home, and came to the front door to greet Aunt Augusta.

"Hello!" he said. "Picked up William on the way?"

He spoke without enthusiasm. He wasn't a mercenary man, but this was his only rich unmarried aunt, and he'd hoped that she wouldn't see too much of William on her visit.

239

Aunt Augusta at once began to pour out a long and confused account of her adventure.

"And we were *completely* lost . . . right in the heart of the wood. I was too much exhausted to go a step farther,

"WE WERE COMPLETELY LOST, RIGHT IN THE HEART OF THE WOOD," SAID AUNT AUGUSTA. "BUT THIS DEAR BOY WENT ON TO EXPLORE."

but this dear boy went on to explore and, solely on my account because I was nervous of our being separated, he tore up his school report to mark the trail. It was, of course, a great sacrifice for the dear boy, because he was looking forward with such pride and pleasure to watching you read it."

William gazed into the distance as if he saw neither his father nor Aunt Augusta. Only so could he retain his expression of patient suffering.

WILLIAM GAZED INTO THE DISTANCE AS IF HE SAW NEITHER
HIS FATHER NOR AUNT AUGUSTA.

"Oh, he was, was he?" said Mr Brown sardonically, but in the presence of his aunt forebore to say more.

During lunch, Aunt Augusta, who had completely forgotten her exhaustion and was beginning to enjoy the sensation of having been lost in a wood, enlarged upon the subject of William and the lost report.

"Without a word and solely in order to allay my anxiety, he gave up what I know to be one of the proudest moments one's schooldays have to offer. I'm not one of those people who forget what it is to be a child. I can see myself now handing my report to my mother and father and watching their faces radiant with pride and pleasure as they read it. I'm sure that is a sight that you have often seen, dear boy?"

William, who was finding his expression of virtue hard to sustain under his father's gaze, took refuge in a prolonged fit of coughing which concentrated Aunt Augusta's attention upon him all the more.

"I *do* hope he hasn't caught a cold in that nasty damp wood," she said anxiously. "He took *such* care of me, and I shall never forget the sacrifice he made for me."

"*Was* it a good report, William?" said Mrs Brown with tactless incredulity.

William turned to her an expressionless face.

"We aren't allowed to look at 'em," he said virtuously. "He tells us to bring 'em home without lookin' at 'em."

"But I could tell it was a good report," said Aunt Augusta. "He wouldn't admit it but I could *tell* that he *knew* it was a good report. He bore it very bravely but I saw what a grief it was to him to have to destroy it—" Suddenly her face beamed. "I know, I've got an idea!

Couldn't you write to the headmaster and ask for a duplicate?" William's face was a classic mark of horror.

"No, don't do that," he pleaded, "don't do that. I-I-I," with a burst of inspiration, "I shun't like to give 'em so much trouble in the holidays."

Aunt Augusta put her hand caressingly on his stubbly head. "*Dear* boy," she said.

William escaped after lunch, but, before he joined the Outlaws, he went to the wood and ground firmly into the mud with his heel whatever traces of the torn report could be seen.

It was tea-time when he returned. Aunt Augusta had departed. His father was reading a book by the fire. William hovered about uneasily for some minutes.

Then Mr Brown, without raising his eyes from his book, said, "Funny thing, you getting lost in Croome Wood, William. I should have thought you knew every inch of it. Never been lost in it before, have you?"

"No," said William, and then after a short silence:

"I say . . . father."

"Yes," said Mr Brown.

"Are you – are you really goin' to write for another report?"

"What sort of a report actually *was* the one you lost?" said Mr Brown, fixing him with a gimlet eye, "Was it a very bad one?"

William bore the gimlet eye rather well.

"We aren't allowed to look at 'em, you know," he said again innocently. "I told you we're told to bring 'em straight home without looking at 'em."

Mr Brown was silent for a minute. As I said before, he wasn't a mercenary man, but he couldn't help being

243

glad of the miraculously good impression that William had made on his only rich unmarried aunt.

"I don't believe," he said slowly, "that there's the slightest atom of doubt, but I'll give you the benefit of it all the same."

William leapt exultantly down the garden and across the fields to meet the Outlaws.

They heard him singing a quarter of a mile away.

Richmal Crompton
Just William on Holiday

"No one stops them *enjoying themselves,"* muttered William. *"They go about havin' a good time all the time, but the minute* I *start they all get mad at me!"*

Holidays are supposed to be a time for rest and recreation. But somehow none of the Brown family seem to spend much time relaxing with William around!

Whether he's rescuing a damsel in distress, sailing the high seas to discover an uncharted island, or capturing a dangerous smuggler on the beach, William never fails to turn his holidays into chaotic adventures that no one will *ever* forget.

Richmal Crompton
William at War

In the dark days of the Second World War, everyone in Britain must do their bit to help defeat the enemy.

William is determined to offer his services to his country – whether it wants him or not. But to the Outlaws' surprise, their enthusiastic contribution to the war effort is hardly ever appreciated . . .

Here are ten hilarious stories about William – at war!

'Probably the funniest, toughest children's books ever written.'
Sunday Times

A selected list of JUST WILLIAM titles available from Macmillan

The prices shown below are correct at the time of going to press. However, Macmillan Publishers reserve the right to show new retail prices on covers which may differ from those previously advertised.

RICHMAL CROMPTON

Just - William	0 333 53408 5	£3.99
More - William	0 333 66226 1	£3.99
William Again	0 333 66227 X	£3.99
Still - William	0 333 37389 8	£3.99
Just William - As Seen on TV	0 333 62802 0	£3.99
William at War	0 333 63793 3	£3.99
Just William at Christmas	0 333 67104 X	£3.99
Just William on Holiday	0 333 65401 3	£3.99
Just William at School	0 333 71235 8	£3.99

All Macmillan titles can be ordered at your local bookshop or are available by post from:

Book Service by Post
PO Box 29, Douglas, Isle of Man IM99 1BQ

Credit cards accepted. For details:
Telephone: 01624 675137
Fax: 01624 670923
E-mail: bookshop@enterprise.net

Free postage and packing in the UK.
Overseas customers: add £1 per book (paperback)
and £3 per book (hardback).